MW01168482

I Pick You

By Stephany Nicole

Acknowledgments

This is where I'd like to say a special thank you to those who were involved in making my dream become a reality. I'd like to thank Dan Adrian, my editor and most importantly, my friend, for your patience and knowledge to make this happen. Thank you to his wife, my best friend of 33 years, who supported me for this and for everything I've been through in my life. Thanks to Cindy Goulding and her team of excellent narrators who made the book come to life in the audible book. To my mom, I love you and appreciate everything that you do for me. To my beautiful children, who are my inspiration, thank you for being the best children a mother could ask for. To my friends and family, thank you for all your support and feedback.

Chapter 1

Why is it, that in almost every movie or book you read, it's raining at a funeral? Is it because rain makes you feel sad? The drops remind you of tears? That death hurts every bone in your body just like a rainy day? Maybe that's how it is in the Hollywood films, or maybe even some in real life. That's how it was when my daddy died. It rained hard that day, poured down on us like a bucket dumped from heaven. That rain hurt. It hurt like hundreds of bee stings all over my entire body. But this time, it's different. The only people here for this one are me and Bella. Oh, and the priest who's giving the sermon. And one other guy who I think Jeffery worked with. His own momma didn't even show. Because she knew the kind of man Jefferey was. Braydon didn't even come. He hated Jeff from the start. After him and Bella's dad left, Bray just wasn't the same. Bella was too little to remember, but she always wanted a father. Jefferey Clark fooled us all. He was a true narcissist in every sense of the word. But I never in my wildest dreams imagined he would die in a car crash. Ok, maybe in a few of my wildest dreams. But I never thought it would actually happen. And yet, there he is ... entombed in a hard plastic case sleeping 6 feet under. It was extremely easy not to shed one tear. Why? Because I knew he couldn't hurt us anymore. And ironically, it was a beautiful sunny day with not a cloud in the sky. I couldn't help but smile, but only on the inside. It just felt wrong to make such a display, so I kept it to myself. When it was over, which didn't take long, I grabbed Bella's hand and started heading toward the car.

"It's such a nice day, isn't it?" I asked Bella after several awkward minutes of silence.

"It sure is. In more ways than one." She answered in her sweet, sarcastic tone.

"Now come on. That's not nice." I replied then finished with a smirk saying "True, but not nice." which made both Bella and I giggle a little. She certainly is smart for a 9-year-old.

We listened to some of our favorite songs as we drove home, which was settled in Boulder, Colorado. We couldn't do that if Jeff was in the car. But I promise I'm not going to complain about him this entire time. It's just nice to be able to do things without walking on eggshells every second of every day. And for the first time in a long time, I felt a sense of calm. A soft smile adorned my face as I listened to sweet, little Bella's voice trying to sing all the words to the songs on the radio. Just a few minutes pass and we pull into our driveway alongside our little home in the middle of nowhere. I went into Braydon's room where he pretty much lives now. I tapped him on the shoulder since calling his name wouldn't do any good. He turned around and took off his headphones and asked, "How was it?"

"It was...." I started, then paused for a moment. I wasn't sure how to answer. If I said it was wonderful, I would sound like a crazy person. If I said it was sad, I would be lying through my teeth. "...it was...how I expected." I finally replied.

Braydon looked at me with a face of irritation then said "Well, I'm glad he's gone." and started to put his headphones back over his ears.

"Hey..." I said as I stopped him. "He may have been a bad guy, but we never want to stoop to his level of evil and wish death on anyone."

Braydon rolled his eyes and continued playing his game. I sat there for a minute just staring at his computer screen feeling like such a hypocrite. There were many nights I laid in bed sobbing from hours of him belittling me, or threatening us, hoping he'd disappear. But I think that's normal when you're in that much emotional turmoil. I got off his bed and headed toward the kitchen where I found Bella looking in the fridge for a snack.

"I'm about to make supper, so don't eat anything." I told her.

"Can I help?" She asked.

I smiled as to say 'yes' and we started looking for something to make. There was some ground beef in the fridge, a jar of sauce and some noodles in the pantry, like there always was.

"I guess it's spaghetti." I spoke.

She was excited. I started teaching her how to make the meatballs and boil the pasta. She asked Alexa to play some music and we danced while cooking. It was nice. No one to criticize us or make fun of us. No one to scream to turn down the music. No one to complain about eating spaghetti again. No one to raise their hands to our faces. It was just pure bliss and absolute peace. As we all sat down to eat, we discussed our day and how we were feeling. It was wonderful to see Braydon smile and make jokes again. It's been so long that I almost forgot what that sounded like. Then he unfortunately brought up a memory with Jefferey in it.

"I think the only good thing about him was he taught Bella how to swim." Braydon said sarcastically. We all kind of giggled. Then Bella's face turned sour.

"What's wrong sweet pea?" I asked her, using a nickname I always call her.

"I miss grandma's pool." She answered.

"Just her pool?" Braydon asked jokingly while snickering.

"No, I miss grandma too." She said as she playfully smacked Braydon in the arm.

"I miss her also." I added.

Then, a sudden thought came over me. Maybe we can move back to my hometown? Maybe we can start over? I mean, I grew up there and was raised there, so it wouldn't be a completely new beginning. But it would be for the kids. And we'd be close to family. The more I thought about it, the more sense it made. I would call momma tonight without letting the kids know just yet. We finished our dinner then Braydon got up to unload the dishwasher. Bella wiped the table while I cleaned the dishes. As I stood in front of the sink with my hands wet from the soapy water, I smiled thinking about the possibility of a fresh start. I was excited and nervous cause Nashville was such a small town. No, not

Nashville, Tennessee. Boy, do I wish. Nashville, Indiana. Bet you didn't even know that existed. There's only 800 people in the whole city, and my momma was still one of the permanent residents. Later that night, after I put Bella to bed and Braydon was back in his room, I called momma to run the idea by her.

"I think it's a fantastic plan." She said in a positive tone.

"You think so?" I asked with doubt in my voice.

"Of course." She replied. "The kids were never happy there and frankly neither were you. After your dad died, it has become more and more difficult to keep up with this big ole house by myself. You could help me at the shop and Braydon can help fix some things."

"Braydon? Fix things? " I stated. "He never leaves his room."

"Well, then it'll be good for him." momma added. "It'll be good for all of you."

She told me to sleep on it and get some rest. We hung up the phone and I already knew I didn't need to sleep on it. This city, this house, the friends I had made, they all remind me of Jefferey. They even remind me of Mitch, the kid's father. He walked out on us when Bella was only 4 months old. She was too little to recall, but Braydon was there to witness the arguing and the breaking of furniture, the drugs and the drinking. I haven't had the best track record when it comes to men. So this was an easy decision for me to make. Moving would mean I could work on me, I could help Braydon come out of his shell even more, give him and Bella the life they deserve. It may be a small town, but it's like a large family full of love. And I couldn't wait to tell them in the morning. I lay there in bed and all these thoughts raced through my mind. I have to sell the house, I have to start packing, I have to quit my job, notify the schools. So much to do and for once in my life, I'm in a good place mentally and have the energy to get things done. I also have a really good feeling about this. A really, really good feeling.

Chapter 2

"How much longer?" Bella asked out of pure boredom and frustration.

"Just a few more hours." I replied.

She rolled her eyes and turned her head to lay it on Braydon's shoulder. He was just staring out the window and had been since the sun came up. We left pretty early in the morning and by now it was closer to supper time. He must have been exhausted as I was too. I kept looking back and forth between him and the road until I finally decided to ask, "You ok champ?"

He slowly turned his head to me and softly replied "Yea." then quickly turned his head back towards the window. I felt like he was mad at me. Or perhaps he's in denial, like he can't believe we finally left that place. Or maybe he's just sad because our life has been one big rollercoaster ride after another. And if he is anything like me, he's had time to reflect on that life this entire 18-hour trip in this smelly, old, beat up, rusty, loud moving van. I couldn't help but wish I could snap my fingers and go back in time, to make things right, to do things different. I found myself hypnotized by the dotted lines on the road as they went by in perfect rhythm. I started to lose myself, wanting to be anyone but me. But then, all of a sudden, Bella jumps up and says, "We're here!"

I snap myself out of wherever I was, just in time to see the welcome sign along Route 46. For miles we saw nothing but forest and cracks in the road. So, it was a sigh of relief to see "Brown County .... Welcome." It would only be a few more turns and I'm at the front door of my childhood. Braydon sat up and we both looked at each other with almost the same thought of 'Here we go'. The closer we got to the center of town, the more people we saw walking and just staring, wondering who we were, questioning why these strangers are coming into their close nit town. I couldn't wait to make that last right turn that will take us on a winding road all the way to mommas' house, nestled among the trees that line Millers Lake. Those last few moments before we arrived seemed to take longer than that entire trip. I wasn't sure why though. Maybe because it was a road that led me down memory lane. Or maybe now it's a road that leads to nowhere. Or maybe it finally leads to somewhere great. Only time will tell.

Finally, we pull around the bend and to no surprise there was momma, sitting in her favorite chair inside her garage with the door wide open. As we pull in the driveway, she rose to her feet and her face lit up with joy. It's been years since she's seen the kids and me. And through no fault of her own. Jefferey made our lives a living hell. He literally controlled who we talked to, where we went, who we could see, and momma was not on that list. But this was it. The second I park this truck and open my door, I become a new me. I'm not that woman anymore, that woman who was under his control. The woman who was now free of his demise and the woman who is starting a new life. So, I put the truck in park, took a deep breath and slowly opened the driver side door. But before I could even place one foot on the ground, Bella had leaped over Braydon to exit the vehicle and run to mommas' arms.

"Grandma!!" she explained as she wrapped her little arms around momma's waist.

"Oh, there's my sweet Angel." Momma said as she hugged Bella tight.

Braydon was casually walking towards momma when she caught sight of him and gasped.

"And who is this fine-looking young man?" she asked as she stretched out her arms to offer an embrace.

Bray wasn't one to hug people. Especially family. But after he paused for a moment, he quietly said, "Hi grandma" and gave her the sweetest hug I've ever seen from that boy. It was almost as if he too was letting go of the past and welcoming his future with open arms. I smiled as momma and I caught eyes and mine began to gradually fill with tears. Momma smiled back, held out her arms and said, "Welcome home baby." I ran to her arms and there we all stood, snuggled tightly together, and it did feel like home. We all let go and with one arm around my shoulders, momma led us to the house that looked exactly how I remembered it. The house I called home the first 18 years of my life. We all headed inside with big smiles on our faces. The house was warm and cozy, everything looked pretty much the same. There were a few upgrades that I assume happened after I moved out. But it was home none the less. The only difference was it was practically empty.

"Momma, where is all the furniture?" I asked perplexed.

"Well," she began, "after your dad died, I got rid of a lot of things. It took me a few years, but I donated most of his stuff to charity. Some is still in the garage. But most of it is in the cottage next to it where I'll be living. You and the kids can move in here."

"Momma!" I exclaimed with excitement in my voice.

"I don't need all this room." she said as she came to hug me. "This is for you and the kids to make it your home now. I have everything I need." She smiled as she looked me in the eyes then we hugged. The kids' faces lit up with elation and momma told them to pick out their rooms. They both quickly darted toward the hallway and started bickering over which room was going to be whose.

"Thank you, momma." I said as I looked at her sweet face.

Just then, Bella came running in from the backyard pretty upset.

"What happened to the pool?" Bella shouted.

I looked at momma confused. But before momma even had a chance to respond, a familiar yet annoying voice screeched loudly behind me saying....

"Well I'll be dipped and rolled in cracker crumbs. If it isn't miss Mary Beth Harper back from the dead."

Peggy Sue Evans. What can I say except she was your typical southern bell, captain of the cheerleading squad, pretty as a peach as they say, an old friend from high school who I haven't seen since Mitch and I moved out of this town. I turned around and there stood this chubby little girl with a belly the size of Texas, hair all a mess and about ready to pop. And by the way, my name is actually Elizabeth Mary Harper. I changed it back to my maiden name after Jeffrey and I got divorced. But something about them southerners with their double names and charming etiquette made everyone call me Mary Beth. When I moved away with Mitch, I always introduced myself as Elizabeth Harper. Most people called me Beth. That was it.

"Peggy Sue Evans." I responded as I looked her up and down. "You look great."

"Thanks. I guess I still have that pregnancy glow." She said with a huge grin on her face as she rubbed her protruding stomach. I shook my head in agreement and asked "So....what brings you by?"

"Well momma Harper here said you was coming back in town. We said we'd offer to help you get settled in." Peggy Sue stated with her distinct southern accent. "Well, not me obviously. I can't lift a 5 lb. bag of sugar right now without feeling like I'm gonna pop right here on the hard wood floor."

"Then who is w.." I started to ask 'who is we?' when suddenly, breezing thru the door way like an old 80's movie with the sunlight dancing behind him and everything moving in slow motion, was Billy Joe Thompson. His big blue eyes were looking right into mine. It took me back to a time when I felt some sort of way for this man. We dated in high school, but I broke up with him when I met Mitch, who was visiting one summer at his grandmas' farm here in Indiana. Maybe that was a mistake. Maybe this was my reason for moving home. Maybe...

"Hi Mary Beth." Billy Joe said with his sexy, sultry voice.

I must have been staring and had a dumb founded look on my face because as soon as he walked over to where we were standing, Peggy Sue put her tiny little hands around his beautiful, big biceps and flashed that one carat diamond ring matched with a wedding band beside it.

"Billy Joe and our son Bobby Flynn are gonna help move you all in." She said with a sassy tone. I was in disbelief and apparently still staring cause momma nudged me and said "We appreciate you all coming to help. Beth? Why don't you show them where everything goes." Then this teenage boy who looked just like Billy Joe came in from outside carrying a heavy box.

"Oh, this is Bobby Flynn. Our son." Peggy said.

"Where does this go?" He asked as momma looked to see it was marked 'kitchen'. Me, still in shock, just stood there. Momma looked at me, then at Bobby and said "Here, it goes in the kitchen. Follow me."

As I came to my senses, I smiled at momma, chuckled awkwardly and began to show Billy Joe to each of the rooms. I just watched him and his son placing boxes and furniture on the floor. 'So, Billy Joe and Peggy Sue got married and had a kid' I thought. And they have one on the way. I guess it made sense. He was the captain of the football team and the cutest boy in school. Gosh my life sounds like a cliché hallmark film. But regardless, that was my life. Later that day, as I carried a box into what would be my bedroom, I placed it on the closet floor and noticed a small box tucked in the corner. When I opened it, there inside was a ton of old pictures. Pictures of me and Peggy in our cheer uniforms. Pictures of me and Billy at our Junior prom. There were some of me and Mitch on our wedding day, mom and dad, the kids when they were babies. They made me start to think of how differently my life might have been if I hadn't met Mitch.

When Mitch Herriot came to visit in the summer of '97, Billy Joe and I had been fighting for a long time. We'd been together since we were 14 and things were just becoming difficult. But we were just kids. He was always playing football and out with the team. I was more interested in going to college and seeing the world. Mitch swept me off my feet. He was a Berkley student studying Bioengineering and I was smitten. He would talk smart and tell me things he had learned and seen. I wanted to be a part of that life. He was older and full of experience. I broke up with Billy to be with Mitch that one hot summer. He came back to visit more often after that. And once I graduated high school, I moved to California to move in with him. We ended up getting married shortly thereafter. But our marriage was rocky from the start. He would attend his classes and I was taking some at the local community college to be a pastry chef. Momma was a baker and I wanted to follow in her footsteps. He graduated college in 2003 and got a job in Boulder Colorado as a Bio Engineer and that's where we bought our first home. But we always argued. And he would rather spend time with his buddies then home with me. About one year later, I got pregnant with Braydon on purpose, thinking it might ground Mitch a little. But after Bray was born, things seem to get worse. He was always at work or out with the guys from work. He would come home drunk or high as a kite almost every week. Sometimes our fights ended in broken furniture or holes in the wall. But I never told anyone. I was too embarrassed. Not even momma knew back then. I would try to make the best of it and did everything I could for both him and Bray. He didn't want Bray in daycare, so I became a housewife and a stay-at-home mom. I put my career on hold to take care of Bray. I constantly felt like nothing I did was good enough for Mitch. He had this great job and I was just a mom. I started going back to work full time as a secretary in an office once Braydon started school and Mitch seemed to appreciate me more as a working mother. Probably because I could make my own money. It felt like things were going to improve. But then in 2012, I got pregnant with Isabella. 4 months later, Mitch left us. He realized he needed to 'find himself' and he's been looking ever since. When Bella was 2, he signed over his rights to both the kids. Then we got divorced in 2015 and I quickly rebounded with Jefferey.

Since I got the house in the divorce, Jefferey moved in with us pretty soon after we met. The first year seemed like a dream come true. He pretended to be everything I ever wanted in a man. But 3 weeks after we eloped, he turned into a completely different person. He was mean, belittling, abusive both mentally and physically. I endured that for 5 years until I finally had the nerve to kick him out. He made our lives a living hell though even after he moved out. He stalked us and threatened us every chance he could. He was a computer guy, so he learned to hack into my social media accounts and emails. I never felt safe. I even changed my name back to Harper since he only knew me as Beth Herriot. Until that day 3 months ago when we learned he had died in a fatal car crash. That was what led me here.

"Hey there." Peggy Sue said as she knocked on the bedroom door.

"Hey." I replied.

"You doin' ok? We're about done bringing in everything." Peggy stated.

I paused for a moment, put the picture I was holding back in the box, and smiled.

"Yea," I said softly, "I'm ok."

Peggy smiled back and added "I'm sorry for whatever you went thru. But I'm sure glad you're here. Maybe it can be like ole times again."

I nodded my head 'yes' and she smiled. She started to walk away when she stopped and said "Oh, I almost forgot. You remember Laura Lynn, Billy Joe's sister." I nodded my head 'yes', and she continued. "Well, her and I and some of the other girls are meeting at Hobnobs Corner for lunch tomorrow to check out the new eye candy. Some guy just moved into town and Brenda May says he comes in every weekday at 11:30 to get a cup a Joe and a slice of your mommas' famous pecan pie. But word on the street is he's finer than a frog hair split four ways." We both laughed and then she asked, "You want a join? You're the only single gal out of the bunch so who knows, maybe you'll get lucky."

I almost started to say no when she begged, "Please?" and gave me the saddest puppy dog eyes ever.

"Sure." I said caving.

She clapped her hands and exclaimed "Yay" then said she'd see me to tomorrow and left. I let out a sigh and looked at all the boxes that were scattered all over my room. Bella came in and told me momma had grabbed some dinner from Big Woods. So, I went down the hall and sat at the table. We were all there. Me, Bella, Braydon and momma, eating pizza and feeling happy, excited for this next chapter in our lives. As I listened to the kids joke and reminisce with momma, I smiled to myself and thought about how life would be for us here. I pictured us having many nights just like this, all together, eating dinner, telling stories and feeling joy. I started thinking about seeing all my old friends tomorrow and being reminded of something Peggy said, 'I'm the only single gal here'. But that's ok, right? After all, I'm here to work on me. I'm here to help the kids forget about the bad times and make good memories. And then I started thinking about this fine-looking eye candy we were going to be seeing. Wonder who that is? Maybe I can have a little fun on my self-recovery. Is that such a crime?

Chapter 3

"Wake up mom." I heard Bella say as she kept nudging me over and over to get up.

"Mom, come on. I start my new school today." she continued.

I really was hoping she would wait until we got settled in. We just got here last night, and I have no clue where anything is. But she just loves school so much and was excited to attend the same elementary school I went to as a kid.

"Mom!" she exclaimed.

"Ok, I'm up." I said a little irritated.

I just wanted to sleep some more since my brain kept me up all night. I kept thinking about Billy Joe and Peggy Sue having a baby and being a family. I thought about working at the bakery with momma. I worried about Braydon not making any friends because he's just so shy. I slowly dragged my legs out of bed one by one, rubbed my eyes and stood up. I followed Bella down the hall and saw Bray still sleeping as I peeked through the crack of his door. I softly asked, "Hey, are you starting school today too?" He grumpily said "No" and rolled over putting the pillow over his head. I slowly shut his door and worked my way into the kitchen. There was momma making breakfast and it smelled so good.

"Well good morning." She said to us.

"Morning." Bella replied.

"Morning." I added as I went to pour a cup of coffee.

"How'd you sleep?" momma asked.

I yawned and said "I slept alright, I guess. Got a lot on my mind."

"I bet you do." momma said.

"I slept like a baby." Bella told us.

Momma and I chuckled as she put eggs on Bella's plate. We sat down at the table and we talked about our plans for the day while we ate breakfast. I told momma I was gonna register Bella in school and meet the girls for lunch. I mentioned that Bray wasn't starting today and that I would take a few days before I helped her in the shop. I just wanted to unpack and make her home feel more like our home.

To be honest, I was really looking forward to going to Hobnobs Corner today. It's been several years since I've thought about a man romantically. Not that I want to dive into a relationship as soon as I got here. But it doesn't hurt to look, right? After breakfast, Bella and I got ready to head out to Van Buren Elementary School, home of the Tigers. About a quarter till 8, I yell out to momma,

"Hey momma, can I borrow your car?"

A few seconds later she comes up to me and hands me a set of keys. I looked at them in shock. I knew exactly what they were for.

"Are you sure?" I asked momma.

"Your father wouldn't want it any other way." She said while smiling.

I hugged her and looked at Bella with excitement. We walked with haste to the garage, opened the door, and there parked inside was dads royal blue 1969 Chevy Sting Ray Corvette. That was his baby. I think he loved that car more than anyone. Bella and I got in the car and I slowly slid my fingers along the cool, leather steering wheel. 'Oh yea, this is gonna be good.' I said to myself. I revved the engine then zoomed out of the driveway. Bella let out a "woo hoo" and we were on our way. We drove down Jefferson Street with the windows down and the wind in our hair. It felt like it was going to be a great day.

As I turned onto Main Street, we saw the shops along the road waking up. People were starting to fill the streets to begin their day. It was a sunny yet cool day in November and the leaves had changed colors. It reminded me of the changes that our family was going through. Getting rid of the old to welcome the new. About 15 minutes pass and we arrive at the school. It looked exactly the same and it brought back so many memories of momma dropping me off every morning. Daddy would usually pick me up on his way home from work and we'd spend the rest of the day working on this very car that I'm driving. Well, he would work on it. I would watch. He'd try to teach me about engines and carburetors. But I couldn't tell you a single thing he said. I just enjoyed spending time with him. He made me laugh. He had the best jokes. After getting Bella registered and settled in her new classroom, I took a stroll down the schools' hallways, running my fingers along the lockers that only the older kids could use. You could see the rust on the doors, but the locks were all new. The tiles on the floor were chipped and the paint on the walls was fading. I smiled to myself and thought 'Just how I remembered it.'

After leaving the school, I went for a drive down highway 135 with the music blaring and my hand out the window. I went into the park we used to play in and decided to stop for a bit. I sat on the swings and just took it all in. I remembered when I met Billy Joe on this very swing. We were in 1st grade and his family had just moved into town. His grandpa had died and his parents inherited the house. That's how they came to be here in Nashville Indiana. I was just about 7 years old with long curly hair and freckles on my face. I was sitting on the swing feeling sorry for myself cause no one wanted to play with me. Then came little Billy Joe introducing himself and asked if he could give me a push. We became best friends after that. Peggy Sue saw that we were always together and became really jealous. Apparently when she was little, she had a crush on him. But she always told me she didn't because she and I were friends too. But then it became a trio. We went everywhere and did everything together. I had my first kiss by Billy Joe when I was 11 years old on the slide by the monkey bars. In exchange, he got a good punch in the nose. But we laughed about it when we got older. We became official at age 14 and he became my first love. Feels like it was just yesterday.

I swung there for about an hour just reminiscing. Then I decided to go to IGA's and get some things for home. I walked down the aisles carrying my basket, taking my time and looking at different items. I was just trying to kill some time before I met the girls at Hobs. But just then, as I contemplated my purchase, this beautiful and tall hunk of a man walked through the doors of IGA. He was literally tall, dark and handsome. I couldn't help but stare because I have never seen anyone who looked that good up close before. As I pretended to read the label of whatever-it-was I was holding, I watched him grab a basket and started walking towards my way. I tried to hide behind the display, but he saw me. Our eyes locked and he smiled. Oh my goodness, his smile. He nodded his head and began going about his business. But he turned around and smiled at me again as he walked down the next aisle over. I must have been blushing. He looked like he was in his 20's. 'Oh if only I was younger'. I said to myself. After I finally collected my mouth off the floor, I continued my shopping trip. As I started to check out, I heard yet another familiar voice.

"Is that Mary Beth Harper?" asked the cashier.

I looked up and saw Kaley Ray Smitter, looking old and heavy set. Not like I remember her.

"Oh, hey Kaley Ray. I can't believe you still work here." I said.

"Been here 26 years last April." She replied.

We chit chatted a bit as she rang up my things. I paid her, grabbed my bags and went on my way saying, "It was good to see you."

While walking toward the car, I saw him again, putting a bag in the back of a white pickup truck. He noticed me and smiled, and I tried to act cool while unlocking my trunk.

"This your car?" He asked surprised.

"Yes." I replied. That was all my mouth could speak cause he was just so pretty.

"69 Stingray. Impressive." he said.

I smiled and attempted to quickly get in the car and die of embarrassment. I sat there for a second and just froze. I was actually starting to sweat. I felt like a 16-year-old girl who just talked to her crush for the very first time. He stood by my car and I didn't move. He smiled, then waved and proceeded to get in to his truck. 'Seriously Beth." I said to myself as I started my car shaking my head. I watched him drive away and I sighed. I wondered if I'd ever see that pretty face again. I couldn't wait to tell the girls and it was about that time to head over to Hobnobs Corner. When I walked in the door of the cafe, I saw Peggy Sue, Sue Ellen, Laura Lynn, and Virginia Lou. Peggy caught sight of me and waved me over. All the girls were happy to see me, and I made my rounds giving everyone hugs.

"You're just in time for the main event." Sue Ellen said.

"Mmhmm. He should be walking through them doors any minute now." Laura Lynn added.

I started to ask everyone how they were and what was new while we waited.

"Well you already know I'm about to pop." Peggy Sue said.

"How does Bobby Flynn feel about another kid being added to his babysitting job?" asked Laura Lynn in a joking manner.

"Another kid?" I asked confused.

"This will make number 5." Said Sue Ellen.

My eyes must have been as big as saucers and I was about to say something clever, but Virginia Lou muttered some words under her breath while fixated on the door to the cafe.

"Oh my god, he's here." she said.

All the girls turned their attention towards the entrance. When I looked up to see who they were all gawking at, guess who was walking through the doors. It was him, the man I just saw at IGA's supermarket. My eyes lit up and my jaw dropped open. Actually, all of us girls looked about the same at that very moment. He saw me and smiled. I just sat there like a deer in headlights and intently watched him walk over to the counter. As he leaned forward onto the bar top, he looked over at me again and smiled once more. All the girls at the table were frozen in amazement. Then they all screeched and immediately started teasing me, encouraging me to get his name and number. They were saying things like 'He looked right at you.' and 'Oh girl, have some fun'

"Oh, for lands sake, I'm twice his age." I said ironically in a southern tone.

"That still makes him legal." Peggy Sue stated, and the rest of the girls laughed.

All they could talk about was my encounter with that man. I told them how I saw him at the supermarket, and he complimented my daddy's car. A few of the girls said it was fate. But I said he's just a boy who happens to be fine as hell. They laughed and I rolled my eyes but kept glancing over at him every so often. I would watch as he lifted his cup to

his beautiful, soft looking, pink, perfect lips. Every bite of pecan pie was slow and delightful.
Sometimes he would look over and catch me staring and we would both just smile. That smile could easily light up the entire room. But I had to snap out of it. He's more than likely half my age. Maybe even younger. There's no way a young good-looking man like that could ever look at an almost 40-year-old woman like me. Besides, he ate his pie, drank his coffee and left about a half hour after he arrived. On his way out, he turned around to look at me and smiled yet again. I looked away and acted like I didn't see. I continued to just enjoy my time with the girls like the good ole days.

We began to wrap up our lunch about an hour after he left, and we all started to say our goodbyes.

"We should definitely do this on the regular." Peggy Sue said.

"At least until you give birth." Laura Lynn replied.

I told the girls I was gonna order some biscuits to take home to the kids then we hugged, and they left the cafe.

When I walked over to the counter and placed my order, I looked down to see his empty plate and half full cup of coffee. 'Those lips have been all over that fork.' I thought to myself. But then I noticed something on the floor by the bar stool legs. I leaned over to pick it up and it was a wallet. I looked around to see if anyone was watching me then I started to investigate. There was some cash, a few receipts, an old picture of a woman holding a toddler, and then I found his license. His picture looked just as good as the real thing. 'Jacob Tyler Brooks.' I softly said to myself. 'Why hello there Jacob.' I said to myself out loud that time.

"Hello." A voice behind me said and I jumped.

I turned around, and to my surprise, there he was, standing in front of me. And once again, I found myself stunned and couldn't move or speak.

"I realized when I got back to work that I lost my wallet." he started. "I guess it's been found." he finished with a smile. But me? Still nothing. Just aloof with awkward silence.

"Well," he began while clearing his throat, "you know my name. Can I ask yours?"

Finally, some words came out. "Elizabeth Harper."

"Well, Elizabeth Harper," he started but I cut him off and said, "Please, call me Beth."

"Oh, ok Beth. Now we're getting somewhere." he said and I sheepishly grinned as I put my hair behind my ear.

I handed him his wallet and he thanked me. As he put it in his back pocket, he stared into my eyes and asked me, "Would you like to go for a walk?"

I thought about it for a second then replied, "Uh yea, I have a little time." And we proceeded to leave. We started walking down Main Street then made a left on Gould Street which winded around to Artist Drive that led us back to Main. It was only a short walk, but we walked at a slow pace and the conversation just flowed. It went something like this....

"So, Elizabeth Harper who goes by Beth," he began. "How long have you lived here in Nashville, Indiana?"

"Well, I actually grew up here."

"Really?"

"Yea. But I left when I was 18."

"Why?"

"Well, to follow some guy I suppose."

"Where's that guy now?"

I must have looked at him with a confused look on my face cause he continued by saying, "I'm sorry, that's none of my business."

But I stopped him and said, "No, it's ok. The answer is simple. There is no more guy. Hasn't been for quite some time." There was a little bit of silence and all you could hear was the occasional gravel rock grinding under our shoes.

"There was a girl for me once also." He said. "But there's no more girl either."

"How old are you?" I asked.

"You didn't see that on my driver's license?" He replied with a smile.

I quietly laughed with embarrassment. "Sorry about that." I said.

"Nah, its ok. I know I look young. But I'm old enough to have been hurt. What about you?"

"Don't you know you never ask a woman her age?" I said with a flirty grin.

"I'll tell you if you tell me." He responded also with a flirty smile.

We were lost in each other's eyes for a moment when my cell phone rang. It was momma. I better not tell her I'm taking a stroll with a young, mysterious stranger, or she'll have my head.

"Hey momma." I answered.

"Hey baby. I'm sorry to interrupt your lunch. But I closed up early and was wondering if I could pick up Bella from school to spend some time with her." She asked.

"Yes, that would be great. I'm sure she'd love that." I replied.

"Fantastic. I'll let you go. Have fun." She said. Then we hung up the phone. After a couple seconds of silence, Jacob asked me, "Everything ok?"

I stopped and noticed we were almost back to Hobnobs Corner. So, I turned to him and said, "Looks like I have more time than I thought."

He smiled then looked over at his truck parked parallel across the street. He then gazed into my eyes while holding out his hand and asked me, "You wanna go for a ride?"

I was hesitant at first. He's a perfect stranger. But after looking around to see if anyone I knew was looking, I nodded my head 'yes' and took his hand. It felt so exciting. And I could feel the adrenaline start to flow. He led me across the street and opened the door for me. I got in and thought

'This is crazy.' But yet, I didn't get out. I buckled up, gave him one more smile and we were on our way.

"So, who is she?" He asked shortly after leaving.

I looked at him puzzled, then he continued, "Well, I didn't mean to pry. But on the phone, you told your momma 'She'd love that'."

I sat there staring out the front window, reluctant to tell him I have a daughter, let alone 2 kids. I'm not sure why. I just met him. But I finally told him.

"My daughter. My momma asked if she could get her from school today."

He nodded his head and turned his eyes back to the road. I guess I seemed flustered cause he looked back at me and said "That doesn't scare me by the way. I love kids."

"Why on earth would I be worried about scaring you?" I said kind of playful.

"You never know." he responded in a lighthearted way. I shook my head at him and bit my lip. Then I noticed we had been driving for almost 25 minutes.

"Where are you taking me anyhow?" I asked.

"I promise I'm not an ax murderer." He replied.

"That's what all the ax murderers say." I snickered.

Just then, we turned down a dirt road that didn't look like it had a name on a map. It led to a clearing and we pulled up to the edge of Lake Monroe. There was an old wooden bench and no one around. He parked the truck and walked toward the bench which had 2 initials carved in it surrounded by a heart. He stood over by the edge of the lake and he went on to say,

"I found this spot by accident one day. My uncle said he needed me to pick up some supplies off Red Oak Lane. I saw the dirt path and I was curious. This is where it brought me. It's become my secret place where I can come to be alone, to escape realty, ya know?" I shook my head yes because I knew exactly what he meant.

"Come with me." I said as I was the one offering my hand this time. He took a deep breath then put his hand in mine. I led him along the shoreline and through some trees. We climbed over large roots and stepped in a few puddles, until we came to another clearing that had a huge rock half in the water and half out. I stared out into the lake watching the reflection of the sun glistening along the water and started to tell him my story about this place.

"When I was in grade school, my daddy and momma and I would be on the Millers boat and we'd pass this rock every time. I told myself I'd sit on this rock one day. And one day I did. I found it while some of us were exploring one night. But I didn't tell the others. I came back when I was by myself. And it became my secret spot to be alone." Then I paused and looked at him saying, "you know, to escape realty?"

He smiled and casually walked over to where I was standing then said as serious as can be "You know, it's not exactly secret."

We both laughed and I lightly smacked him on the arm in a playful manner. We continued talking about life and music. We seemed to have a lot in common which was strange considering I was so much older than him. Although I really didn't know how old he actually was. But he had to be old enough to have been in love and been hurt. As we strolled along the shoreline, I found myself intrigued by this man. He was young, yes. But he had an old soul. I felt like I'd known him for years and at the same time I knew nothing really about him. Which was exciting in itself.

"You know, I don't even know how long you've lived here or who you know." I began. "I grew up here and I've never seen you before. I mean, I was gone for years but everyone I know who's been here their whole lives don't even know anything about you."

He made a look on his face with a mischievous smirk and I said "Fine, keep your secrets."

"Sometimes people just need time to see if they can trust someone." He said. "When you trust someone, then you can tell them anything they want to know."

"Fair enough." I replied.

I mentioned it was getting close to supper time and he agreed to take me back to my car. The drive back was quiet but we were both grinning from ear to ear. I wondered what he was thinking, and I hoped he didn't wonder the same thing. I kept thinking about how I told myself I wasn't going to jump into a relationship first thing after moving here. I thought I was safe from that because I knew everybody. Or so I thought. We arrived back at Hobnobs Corner and I got out of his truck. I closed the door and turned around to say, "I had a really nice time."

"Me too." He responded.

As I started walking away, he asked if he could have my number. I was reluctant at first but I gave it to him anyway.

"Have a good night, Beth Harper." He said with a soft and gentle voice.

"You too, Jacob Brooks." I responded.

He smiled and drove off and I just stood there watching him leave. I got back in my car but I didn't go right away. I started the engine but I just idled in the parking spot. I sat there and thought about what just happened. Should I tell the girls? Should I tell momma? Should I just keep him my not so dirty little secret? Maybe that's what I'll do. I want to see where this goes. So, for now, I'll just keep things to myself and not get my hopes up. But I sure couldn't stop smiling all the way home. When I pulled into the driveway, I parked the car and gradually worked my way to the front door. When I went inside, to my surprise, no one was home. I kept calling everyone's names. "Momma? Braydon? Bella?" But there was no response. I started walking around looking into everyone's room and no one was there. Finally, I heard little Bella's voice and even Bray was talking and laughing outside the front door.

"Hey, where you guys been?" I asked as they came in the door.

"Oh, you're finally home." Momma said. "That was a long lunch. Did you have fun?"

"Yes, I did. What about you guys?"

"Well, I noticed someone was moving into the old Miller house across the way and I wanted to introduce myself." Momma explained. "The kids wanted to come so we brought them a pie."

"Yea mom," said Bella. "They have a daughter who's 11 and a son who's 7."

"They even have an older son that Bray could get to know." Momma added.

"Really?" I asked, hoping it wasn't Jacob.

"Yea. His name is J.T. He seems really cool." Braydon commented. "He asked me to come hang out tomorrow after school."

"That's awesome Bray." I said relieved. "So, you're starting school tomorrow."

"Yea I think I will." Bray replied.

Momma and I looked at each other like we were impressed. Then she said "Oh, and they invited us over for a cookout on Friday night."

"Sounds fun." I responded.

The rest of the night we spent talking about their days. Bella told me about school and how she loved her teacher. She also said she enjoyed meeting the neighbors and asked if the daughter could spend the night some time. I didn't see a problem with that, and that made her happy. We decided to make some dinner and just enjoyed each other's company. It was the first time in a long time that I heard this much noise from all of us. Especially from Bray. After Mitch left, he fell into a depression. And when Jeffery came along, that made things even worse. He became a recluse and I lost that little boy who used to be a social butterfly so full of life. Maybe making this new friend will help him go back to the Bray I used to know. Which is all the more reason why I should leave my little escapade with Jacob to myself. I want the kids to know I am focused on them 100%. Well, maybe 95%.

Chapter 4

Beep beep. Beep beep.

It was almost 7 am on a Wednesday morning and I kept hearing this sound that wasn't my usual alarm. When I realized it was a text message, I grabbed my phone and thought 'Who is texting me so early?' I looked and saw a number I didn't recognize with a message that said, 'Good morning, Elizabeth Harper.' I laid there for a second not exactly sure who this was until it hit me. 'Jacob?' I replied back. And all he sent was ':-)' So I responded, 'Good morning, Jacob Brooks ;-)' We then texted the entire morning. He told me he had to go into town today for his uncle and wanted to see me again. 'I know it's an hour drive, but could you meet me for lunch at St. Elmo's?'. I thought about how this might not be such a bad thing. St. Elmo's was in Indianapolis. There's no one I know who lives there. And no one from here will see me. I stared at the message for a long time. It was nice to have someone to talk to again. And he sure was handsome. But was this a good idea? 'It's just lunch.'

I thought trying to justify what I was about to do next. So, I smiled and agreed to meet him. Just then momma said, "What are you smiling about?"

"Oh, just a friend wants to have lunch with me today." I responded.

"That's nice." Momma replied. "I'm glad you're gettin' to catch up."

I shook my head and went about my day. After I took everyone to their schools, I came home and started debating on what I should wear. I took a shower and curled my hair. I put on makeup and found a cute little dress to put on. I covered my shoulders with a cardigan, put on my boots and by that time it was almost 11. So, I got in the car and set out for St. Elmo's. My heart started skipping beats. I can't believe this gorgeous young guy wants to see me again. What should I say when I see him? Should I hug him? Should I shake his hand? I started practicing how I would say 'hello' and felt like such an idiot. 'It's just lunch.' I said to myself again. Why am I getting so worked up? That drive seemed to take an eternity. But I finally pulled up to St. Elmo's and saw him standing by his truck, holding a small bouquet of flowers. I parked and took a deep breath then got out and said "Hello."

"Hello Elizabeth Harper." He replied. "You look beautiful."

"Thank you." I said.

He just stared at me grinning then finally said, "Oh, these are for you."

He handed me the bouquet of daisies and mini sunflowers, which were my favorites. I told him that a couple days ago when we were sitting by the lake. It impressed me that he remembered.

"Thank you," I said. "That's so sweet."

I put them in the car, and he held out his arm to escort me. I giggled and put my hand through that arm. He felt strong but not overly muscular. He was about 6 foot and had brown thick hair, the most beautiful blue eyes I had ever seen and a smile that could kill. We went in, got a table and he pulled out my chair for me. He certainly is a gentleman, that's for sure. During lunch we talked about many things. There wasn't a moment where we didn't have something to say. It was so easy to talk to him. And this is how some of it went.

"So does your daughter have any siblings?" He asked.

"Uh, I have a son, too." I replied.

"Nice. I have 2 sisters and one brother myself."

"I'm actually an only child." I mentioned.

I started to tell him a little about my childhood and things that we had been through. I didn't go heavily into detail, but I did tell him about Mitch.

"I'm sorry you had to go through that." He said with compassion.

"It's ok. It was for the best." I replied.

There was a slight pause then he said, "I was engaged before I moved here, to the girl that's no more."

To be honest, I was a little astounded at this. He seemed so young. But then again, I was 19 when I married Mitch.

"What happened?" I asked.

He took a deep breath then said, "She ended up leaving me for my best friend in college."

I felt so bad for him and a little guilty at the same time. I left Billy Joe for Mitch and I knew he was heartbroken. But it all worked out cause look at him now? Married to Peggy Sue and about to have their 5th child. No sooner had I thought that, Jacob continued.

"But it all worked out for the best. If that hadn't of happened, I wouldn't have moved here. And I wouldn't have met you." He smiled and peered into my eyes almost directly into my soul. I smiled and looked down to notice I was fidgeting with my napkin. Why does he have such an effect on me? He's funny and handsome and so sweet. It's like he's too good to be true. But I reminded myself that I wasn't going to jump into anything serious and decided to change the subject.

"So....what made you move here anyways?" I asked.

He proceeded to tell me his moms half-brothers wife passed away and they agreed to help his uncle with the business. He told me his mom was good with bookkeeping like his aunt was and he needed a young back to help with the heavy lifting. But before I could ask 'who is your uncle', the waiter came over to our table and asked if we needed anything else. Jacob looked at his watch and said, "I think just the check."

After the waiter walked away, Jacob told me it was almost 1:30 and he should really get back to what he needed to do. I had to go and pick up Bella in an hour, just the amount of time it would take me to drive back. He insisted on paying for the check even though I offered to pay half. But he didn't let me. This was a nice change and I sure could get used to this. But I started thinking again that this was undeniably crazy. This is a date. I can't be on a date with him. He's way too young. What I am doing? If anyone ever found out, things would never be the same.

We walked to the parking lot and like the gentleman he was, he opened my car door for me. I started the car, rolled down my window and he leaned on the door to say, "I had a nice time again miss Elizabeth Harper." I love how he says my first and last name. I was hypnotized by his eyes and replied, "I did too mister Jacob Brooks." We smiled, he stood up and watched me as I drove away. The whole drive back to Nashville I kept replaying our lunch over and over in my head. He doesn't seem like a young man. And when I'm around him, I don't feel my age either. But I can't allow myself to get too attached. Could we really have a future though? What would the kids think? I wanted Jacob to understand that I wasn't looking for a relationship, but I didn't want to be mean about it. So, I texted him when I got to Bella's school and said, 'I'm glad I met a new friend.' Yes, I put 'friend'. He is my new friend. Nothing more.

After picking up both the kids from their schools and heading home, they told me about their days and what they did.

"I can't believe you have Mr. Fletcher for English." I told Bray. "He was my English teacher when I was in 12th grade.". When we got home, the kids had a snack and I asked Bray, "What time are you hanging out with, J.T. was it?"

"Later on. Maybe after dinner." he replied. He started to eat the sandwich he made and went to his room. Bella asked if we could watch some tv together and I agreed. I kept checking my phone though the entire time. He never texted me back. Maybe the 'friend' comment hurt his feelings. Maybe he just got busy. Maybe I'm overthinking like I always do.

"Are you expecting a phone call?' Bella asked as she saw me constantly looking at my phone.

"No sweet pea." I replied. Then she snuggled into me and smiled. We continued to watch tv, but I wasn't really watching. My mind and heart were just racing. After dinner that night, and while Braydon was doing the dishwasher, he got a message on his phone and said, "Alright mom. I'm gonna hang with J.T." he said as he sped up his chores to get done quicker.

"Ok champ. Have fun." I replied.

I finished cleaning up the kitchen and Bella went back into the living room. She asked me and momma if we wanted to watch a movie. So, we did. I was distracted of course, wondering why Jacob hasn't texted me back. Later that evening, after kissing Bella goodnight, I went into my room and plopped on my bed. I laid there flat on my back staring at the ceiling and noticed the remnants of old glow in the dark stars that apparently don't glow anymore. Kind of resembles how I feel at my age. Except for now. When I'm around Jacob, I just feel young. I rolled over on my side and saw my phone on the table. I picked it up and went to our messages. Nothing yet. This was killing me. Is he playing with me? Is this hard to get? Oh god, did he get home ok? I decided to text him again. I thought about what I was going to say and then what I came up with was, 'Hope you got home safe. It was fun today. But it's probably best we keep that to ourselves.' I turned off my phone and no sooner had I laid it down on the bed, the notification chimed. It was him. His reply was, 'You got it, friend ;-)' I started to type something else, but I wasn't sure what to say next. So, I just left it at that. I set my phone on the table and saw momma had just walked into the room.

"You doin ok?" she asked me as she sat on the edge of my bed.

"Yes, why you ask?" I replied as I sat myself up and skootched my back to the headboard.

"You just seem a little distracted is all." Momma said concerned.

I am distracted, I thought to myself. How can I tell her that I have a crush on a 20 something year old guy? In fact, I really don't know how old he is. I don't know anything about him. He's just a friend who I had lunch with. No big deal, right?

"I just have a lot on my mind." I finally told her.

"I understand," She began, "and I'll always listen if you ever need to empty your head."

"Thanks momma." I responded as I gave her a hug.

"I'm glad you're here." she said while rubbing my back.

"Me, too." I said.

Just then I saw Braydon walking down the hallway.

"Bray?" I said a little loudly.

He walked back towards my door and I continued, "Come sit."

So, momma left, and Braydon took her place. I asked him how his night was and what he did with J.T. He told me they played video games and watched a movie. He reminded me the old Miller's house has a pool and J.T. told him we can go swimming anytime when it gets warmer. It sounded like he had a lot of fun. I was so happy to hear the excitement in his voice to have a friend again. It's been a long time since he's let anyone in. It's been a long time since we sat and talked like this. It seems like the 3 of us had made some nice new friends. And I hope it stays that way. He must be a good kid to be able to bring Braydon out of his shell like that. I can sleep soundly tonight knowing my kids seem like they are finally happy.

Chapter 5

Over the course of the next few days, I watched as Braydon came more and more out of his shell. Bella was making lots of new friends. And life was busy at momma's cake shop. I found myself getting into my groove with balancing work, kids, and spending time with friends. I haven't seen Jacob since our lunch date together. And he hasn't even texted me since the 'friend' comment. I guess that ship has sailed. Not that there really was a ship to begin with. I am looking forward to this evening though. I finally get to meet the new neighbors and see who Bella and Braydon have been spending all their time with. I put the finishing touches on the cake and said to everyone, "Ok. I'm done. We ready to go?"

Momma grabbed her corn souffle, I grabbed my cake, the kids got on their shoes and we walked down the road to the old Miller house. That's where the new neighbors moved in. Malcolm and Tammy Miller were an older couple that had a general store and a lumber yard in town. After his wife died, Mr.

Miller was all alone and had to close the general store. I believe he still runs Nashville Lumber Company but I'm not too sure. It's been so long since I've seen him. He moved into his sons' home so him and his wife could take care of him. But his son owned the Miller's Ice Cream shop down on Main Street and had no desire to sell wood. I remember every summer the Millers would take us out on their pontoon boat and ride across Lake Monroe. That's where I found my little spot of solitude. The house had been empty for years, so it will be interesting to see what the new neighbors have done to the place.

As we walked up the hill on the driveway leading to the front door, I started to remember spending our summers here. Things looked a little different though with a new blue door and new flowers planted on the lawn. The roof was swept of all debris and I could smell the fresh coat of paint. Braydon rang the doorbell and this handsome man and his beautiful wife answered that had to be close to my age.

"Hi there." said the woman. "I'm Caroline and this is my husband, Travis."

"Nice to finally meet you," Said Travis, "Braydon's told us so much about you."

"It's nice to finally meet you, too." I replied.

"Please, come in." stated Caroline.

We walked in to the foyer and there was still some construction going on. The wood floors looked polished, there were paint cans and tarps covering some furniture. The old stone fireplace looked like it had been whitewashed. But it was the old Miller house for sure. Just revamped a little.

"Pardon the mess," Caroline explained. "We're still fixing some things up."

"Let me introduce you to the kids." Said Travis. "Kids!"

A couple seconds later, here comes an adorable little 7-year-old boy and a beautiful 11-year-old girl.

"This is our son, Matthew and daughter, Tonya." Said Caroline.

"It's nice to meet you." They both said in unison.

I smiled and said it was nice to meet them too. Then Tonya asked Bella to come in their room to play and Bella followed with excitement. Just then, I heard someone else's footsteps. I slowly looked up to see who it was and to my surprise ... it was Jacob. He stood next to Caroline and looked at me bewildered.

"Elizabeth?" Jacob said surprised to see me. I looked at him in agitation and shook my head 'no' as inconspicuous as I could.

"How do you know my mom's name?" Braydon asked.

I was still shaking my head 'no' and was hoping he would get the hint that I didn't want anyone to know that we had already met.

"Uh, yea dude, you told me." Jacob said and Braydon acted like he remembered.

I had no idea what just happened, but I needed to get away from this situation fast before I screamed or fainted or both.

"Um, this cake really needs to be in a fridge." I said.

"Oh right. J.T. Can you show her to the kitchen and make some room for it?" Caroline asked.

Jacob shook his head 'yes' and started walking in the other room. We went through a doorway and into the kitchen. He opened the fridge and asked, "How much room do you need me to make?"

"J.T.?" I said confused as I set the cake on the counter.

"Short for Jacob Tyler." Jacob replied after he shut the fridge and slowly turned around.

I shook my head and was still in shock. He leaned against the kitchen counter and crossed his arms.

"What?" He asked.

"What?" I asked back.

"That look. What are you thinking?"

"You are J.T. You and my son. We had lunch. The walk. My secret spot." I stated while pacing.

"Hey." he started. "It's really ok."

"No, it's not ok!" I exclaimed. "If Braydon ever found out...."

"He won't." he interrupted. "Besides, there's nothing for him to find out, remember? We're just friends." he ended with an irritated tone and walked out of the kitchen.

I followed him to the dining room where the table was set, and it smelled heavenly.

"It smells wonderful in here." Momma said with enthusiasm.

"Thank you. J.T. here is the chef tonight." Caroline answered.

We all looked at Jacob stunned.

"Wow." Momma stated utterly impressed.

I just looked at him and smiled with a look of surprise. And he just smiled back while shrugging his shoulders. We all sat down and ironically, I was placed right across from Jacob, with Braydon on my right, and Bella in between my mom and Jacob. Caroline and Travis were sitting at either end. Travis said grace and we started to eat. It was awkward. Jacob kept looking at me over the table. I would try to pretend I didn't notice, but I did. I would look at his beautiful face when he wasn't looking. My momma asked how they got to be here in the old Miller place and Travis started telling the same story Jacob told me at St. Elmo's. The only difference was, Jacob left out all the names.

"So, wait. Your last name is Miller?" I asked Caroline and Travis.

"My maiden name was Miller." Caroline answered.

She then told us how Malcolm was her much older half-brother. Her momma left her dad in Nashville when Caroline was just a baby. Her dad eventually married Mr. Miller's mom when he was 15. So it was no wonder I never heard of her. She said she was 48 and Jacob was a product of her first love, Jonathan Brooks, along with his older sister, Jessica, who still lives in Washington State. Later, she married Travis Concord who was sitting right here and had Matthew and Tonya during their 15 years of marriage.

"After Tammy died," she said, "Malcolm moved in with his son and left this house. He'd been asking us for years to move here and help him with the company. But it was never the right time. When Amanda and J..." she paused and looked at Jacob and finished by saying, "well, J.T. was the one who convinced us to make the move. And I'm so glad we did."

She smiled at him and he smiled back. And it was quiet for a moment. Then to cut the tension in the air, momma blurted out, "Well that was delicious. Great job J.T. Anyone want dessert?"

"I'll get the cake." I said, then went back into the kitchen. Jacob followed me in after saying, "I'll help her find what she needs."

He came into the kitchen and put some of the dirty dishes in the sink that he had gathered from the table. I was just standing there looking at the cake, not knowing how to feel right now.

"Are you ok?" He asked quietly.

I turned around and asked, "Was Amanda your fiancé?"

He nodded his head 'yes'. Then it was quiet again.

"How old are you?" I asked, cause I still wasn't sure.

"What's with you and this age thing?" He replied.

"I wanna know." I responded cutting him off.

He paused for a moment then stated, "I'll be 21 in April."

"Oh my god." I exclaimed.

"Why is that such a big deal to you?" he asked.

I thought to myself, he's only 20. I was speechless. We just looked at each other not knowing what to say. But I knew one thing ... for some reason, this "kid" had an effect on me and I had been trying to ignore it. I literally wanted to go over and kiss him, but I had no idea why. Maybe it's because he was gorgeous? Or maybe because the thought of being with a 20-year-old excites me? But I was angry and confused and upset and so many emotions balled up into one. Thank God momma walked in and saw us just standing there.

"Everything alright in here?" she asked.

"Yes, we were just about to come out." I replied.

I picked up the cake and carried it into the dining room. Momma soon followed. Then Jacob came out a few minutes later holding a knife and small plates. Momma picked up the knife and began serving everyone and we chatted some more about life and the weather.

"Why don't we move this into the living room?" Caroline said after she cleared the table from dessert. Jacob helped her and he took the last bit of dishes into the kitchen while the rest of us transitioned into the other room. As I walked past the fireplace toward the tan suede couch, I noticed an old acoustic guitar on a stand next to the table. I ran my fingers over the strings and asked, "Who plays?"

"I fiddle around with it a little bit." said Travis. "But J.T. is the real musician here."

"I mean, I play a little too." Jacob responded as he slowly walked into the room and leaned against the wall. The guitar reminded me so much of the one my daddy used to play. Sometimes when I was feeling down or even when I was happy, he would play and sing me a song to put a smile on my face.

"Seriously dude?" said Braydon "you play? That's awesome."

"Can you play us a song?" Bella asked.

He tried to say 'no' but everyone in my family tried to convince him otherwise. He finally caved, picked up the guitar and sat on the fireplace hearth. He shook his head, took a deep breath, looked me right in the eye and started playing. It was beautiful I must admit. I just stood there and watched. But then, he opened his mouth and started singing. I slowly inched over to the couch and sank into the cushions. I know that song. I remember daddy used to sing it for momma. I looked over at her and she was just strolling down memory lane, I could see it on her face. I watched as she silently mouthed the words to the song with one lonely tear slowly falling down her cheek. Then I remembered what song it was, Make It With You by Bread. And while Jacob sang it, he was looking at me the entire time, just staring into my eyes like he wrote those words for me. I couldn't believe that tears started to well up in my eyes, but I had to quickly wipe them away. I was amazed at this man. But I couldn't let him know because Braydon was getting attached too. They have been spending a lot of time together so this was going to be extremely difficult. Everyone clapped as he played the last chord. And I just sat there astonished.

"You're gonna have to teach me how to play." Braydon said as he walked over to Jacob and put his hand on Jacob's shoulder.

Jacob looked at me and smiled a compunctious smile then looked up at Braydon. They did their guy handshake and I was just screaming inside. This cannot be happening. I cannot be developing feelings for my sons' friend. Oh god, that even sounded awful in my own head. I would just have to try and keep my distance, play it cool. But how? I just have to keep reminding myself he's only 20 years old.

As the evening came to a close, we all started thanking the Concords for their hospitality. I walked over to Jacob who was standing by the door alone waiting to open it for us. I quietly said to him, "You are just full of surprises, aren't you?"

He looked me in my eyes, then back at everyone else who was working their way toward the door, then back at me. Then he quickly and quietly said to me, "Meet me at our spot. Midnight"

My heart started racing. I assumed he meant the place I showed him with the large rock. We spent our first several hours after meeting each other there just talking. I gently nodded my head in compliance. Braydon came up to Jacob and shook his hand, Momma commented on his talent once more, Bella gave him a hug, and we were on our way home. I kept turning back and smiling, watching the Concords wave at me as I did. Jacob just looked at me with that alluring smile of his. I wondered if he could tell I was awestruck? After we got back home, I said goodnight to Bella after she changed into her pjs and crawled into bed. I went in to Braydon's room and he was laying down watching something on his phone.

"Hey." I said. He looked over at me and waited for me to continue.

"Did you have a good time?" I asked.

"Yea. I told you he was cool." he replied.

"Yea, Yea he is cool." I responded.

"I'm going to go to bed though after this video." Braydon continued. "I'm so tired."

"Alright then. Well, goodnight. I love you." I told him

"Night. Love you too." He responded.

I walked back into the other room and saw momma putting left overs in the tupperware containers. "You going to bed?" I asked.

"Yea, once I put all this stuff away. I'm beat." She responded.

I helped her continue to put things away then once we were finished, she said, "Goodnight baby girl." and walked away to her little cottage. I went to my room and sat on my bed. I kept looking at my phone watching the time. The minutes ticked by slowly and I started to get antsy. Then my brain interjected. 'Why are you doing this? What has gotten into you? Midnight? You never stay up till midnight. You're old. He's so young. Let him be a kid. He's your sons' new friend. You're a terrible person. You can't do this.' Just then, my phone beeped and I received a text message from Jacob. 'You comin?' he asked. So, I impulsively replied, 'On my way.'. I looked out the window and saw headlights riding by. So, I quietly snuck out the front door. I could see his brake lights in the distance down the road. I got in my car and hesitated. This is a V6 engine. It will definitely wake everyone up. I went back into the house and searched for mommas' keys. Her car is a sedan and starts extremely quietly. I found them on the kitchen counter and again quietly snuck out the door. I started the car and sure enough, it was quiet. I backed down the driveway and headed toward Lake Monroe.

During that entire ride, I kept thinking about all the thoughts I had just had back at home. Why are you doing this? Because we're friends, right? Friends can hang out, can't they? Thirty minutes later I reached the lake. I parked my car and had to walk the rest of the way to the spot I knew he was talking about. My spot with the rock. I turned the corner and there he was, standing along the shoreline. He turned around and smiled and said, "Hello friend."

I gave him a sarcastic smirk and walked towards him. As I got closer, I noticed there were 2 folding chairs, some candles in the sand, and one sunflower laying on the seat of the chair.

"Friend huh?" I asked.

"Yes, thank you." he replied sarcastically. "Can't someone do something nice for their friend?"

"Mmhmm." I responded with a questionable tone. He motioned me to sit down and we laughed because he tried to pull out my chair but the sand kept making that difficult. I took my flower and had a seat. He sat down next to me and kept looking at his watch then back at the sky several times.

"What are you looking at?" I asked as I looked up.

"Just watch." he answered as he looked at his watch one last time than back towards the sky.

Then, out of nowhere, the sky lit up with a meteor shower. It was like dozens of shooting stars were dancing across the sky. But my attention quickly turned to Jacob. I watched his face light up as the meteors burned in the atmosphere creating a display of radiant light. He loved this. I loved this. He started telling me about the universe and what happens when a meteor hits the atmosphere. I was mesmerized. I remembered at that moment when Mitch would tell me things he learned in collage. It was fascinating and I hungered for more. But when Mitch spoke, he spoke from the mind. It was just knowledge and things he knew. When Jacob speaks, he speaks from the heart, he speaks with passion. It was beautiful.

The light show lasted about 35 minutes and for the next couple hours after, we just talked under the moonlight and blanket of stars. I must have dozed off because I opened my eyes and saw Jacob sleeping in the chair and me covered in a blanket. I jumped up and yelled, "Oh my god, what time is it?"

I startled Jacob waking him up and he was slightly disoriented. I checked my phone and saw it was 3:27 in the morning. I also saw that I had 4 missed calls and 10 text messages from Billy Joe.

"Oh no." I said out loud.

"What is it?" Jacob asked.

I read the messages and saw that Peggy Sue was having the baby and she wanted me to be there. I told Jacob and we quickly grabbed everything that was there and headed to our cars. As I helped him load up his truck, I said to him, "You can't come with me."

"Wait. Why not?" he asked.

"Cause no one can know that we are friends." I said.

He rolled his eyes while slamming his tail gate and started walking away. So I continued.

"Jacob please. Life is good right now for the kids and I don't want to mess that up."

He just stared at the ground and didn't say a word.

"Please?" I said again sincerely.

"Ok." he said with a melancholy tone.

"Thank you." I said as I got in my car and headed to the hospital.

As I drove down that old dirt road, I could still see Jacob standing there through the rear-view mirror. He didn't leave. He just leaned against his truck watching me drive away. All I could think about was Peggy Sue and not because she was having her baby. I was selfishly worried they called momma, and everyone would find out I wasn't home. This is already becoming such a mess. I feel like a liar and an awful person. As I arrived at the hospital I ran into the entrance and saw a large group of people, most of which I knew. And there was Billy Joe pacing the room while biting his nails. I called his name and he looked over then ran to me and wrapped his arms around me.

"What's going on? Is Peggy Sue ok?" I asked as I scoured the room looking for momma. Fortunately, I didn't see her.

"They took her to the operating room." He started with nervousness in his voice. "Her heartbeat dropped and the baby's heartbeat disappeared."

"Oh my god." I said quietly. I hugged him again and whispered, "She'll be ok. She's strong."

We walked over to the waiting room chairs and people I knew were saying hi. Some I've already seen since I've been back. Some I haven't seen yet. They were surprised to see me and every one of them gave me a hug. After the pleasantries, I went to sit next to Billy Joe who looked extremely worried. As I sat down, he gave me a half assed smile and looked the other way.

"Hey Billy," I began, "Just curious. Why did you call me to come?"

"She asked me to." He replied.

"She did?" I asked surprised.

"She loves you, Mary Beth." he responded.

I looked away and questioned what he just said in my mind. I never kept in touch with her all these years. Why would she want me here? Why would she love me?

"Did you call my momma by any chance?" I asked.

"No," he said, "should I have?"

"Oh no, I was just wondering."

Moments later, the doctor came in, and half the room, including Billy and myself, stood up to hear what he had to say.

"Good news. Mom is stable. She's in recovery. You'll be able to see her in a couple hours." the doctor said.

"And the baby?" asked Billy.

"You have a beautiful new healthy baby girl." the doctor replied with a smile.

The whole waiting room cheered in relief and Billy picked me up off the ground.

"You gonna stick around and see her?" Billy asked with an elated face after he put me back down.

"Of course." I replied.

I sat back down in my seat and watched as Billy made his rounds of embracing everyone and being congratulated. I again dozed off cause about an hour and 20 mins later, I was woken up by my phone ringing.

"Hello?" I answered yawning.

"Where in the hell are you?" I heard momma say on the other line. "Do you have my car?"

"Momma!" I exclaimed "I'm at the hospital. Peggy Sue had her baby."

"Oh, thank heavens you're alright. Braydon went to the restroom and noticed you were gone and he woke me up. Where's my car?"

Quick. Think of something. "I couldn't find my keys, but I saw yours." I answered. And there it was. My first lie. Along with that came the guilt.

"Oh, ok." Momma said, "Well I'm glad you're ok. Give Peggy Sue my love."

I hung up the phone and felt like someone had just stabbed a knife in my stomach. I'm not good at this lying stuff. I better not make a habit of that. Just then, the doctor came back and said Peggy was awake. Billy turned to me and said, "You're family. Come with us."

I got up off my chair and followed him, Peggy's mom, Billy's parents and all 4 of his kids into the room where Peggy was staying. I was the last one to walk in and there she was, sitting in the bed, holding a brand-new baby girl in her arms. I watched as Billy tenderly kissed her forehead and then did the same to the baby. Peggy then gave the baby to Billy and he began talking to her in a sweet daddy voice.

"What's the baby's name?" asked the nurse in the room.

"Elizabeth." Peggy responded, "I named her after my best friend."

She looked at me and smiled. I was beside myself. I can't believe she still considers me her best friend after all these years. Especially considering that I haven't even once called her to see how she was. I have done nothing to earn that title.

"You want to hold her?" She asked me.

Billy walked over to me and gently placed this sweet, adorable baby girl in my arms. It's been a while since I've smelled that newborn smell. But then, I guess the guilt of sneaking around with Jacob, the guilt of lying to momma, the guilt of not being there for Peggy all these years overwhelmed me and I just started crying.

"Can you give us a minute?" Peggy Sue said sweetly to everyone in the room.

As they all walked out of the room, I went over to her bedside and sat down.

"I'm so sorry Peggy Sue" I said while ugly crying, "I never meant to forget you. Truth is I never did forget you. I just got so caught up in my own stupid life that..." and then she interrupted me saying, "I know. You always wanted more than this small-town life. And that's ok. You're here now. You can make it up to me."

We both smiled and I just stared at this little girl in my arms. I slowly handed her back to Peggy and we chatted for a while. By then the sun had come up and I was exhausted. I texted momma to let her know I was on my way back. When I got home, momma was in the kitchen and Bella was watching tv. I told her about the baby and that we could go visit them tomorrow. I went and kissed momma on the cheek while handing her back her keys, then I headed to my room. I fell into the bed face first and laid there for a few seconds. I then rolled over and stared at the ceiling and thought to myself, 'What a day!'. I shook my head and let out a big sigh. I just couldn't wrap my head around everything that had just transpired. But maybe I can think more clearly after I get some sleep. So, I buried myself under the covers, still in my shoes and fell fast asleep.

Chapter 6

Ring Ring. Ring Ring. Ring Ring. Ring Ring.

I quickly sat up in bed frightened by the sound of my phone ringing over and over. I wiped the drool from my lips and answered, "Hello?"

"Where are you?" shouted momma.

"What?" I said all discombobulated.

"You said you'd help me in the shop today!"

As fast as I could, I jumped out of bed, got changed and ran to the car. I told her I'd be on my way as soon as I could. Luckily the bakery is only a few short turns away. When I arrived, the shop was packed with people.

"Sorry." I said as I walked with haste to grab my apron and help. In a rush, I helped momma put the finishing touches on some pastries these people were waiting for. I took pies out of the oven and boxed up the cookies. I felt like a chicken with its head cut off. Apparently, a tour bus got lost driving to Nashville Tennessee and ended up here. So, some hangry tourists were looking for a quick sugar fix. Once the shop died down, I was able to focus on decorating a wedding cake that was for Sunday. As I piped the icing, I heard the chime for the door and turned to see Jacob breezing through it.

"What are you doing here?" I asked in a loud whisper.

"I had to see you..." he started but then momma came out from the back just as he was saying that. "youuuur momma."

"Me?" She asked.

"Yes. Joanna down at Hobnobs Corner said you were the one responsible for their delicious slice of pecan pie. So, I figured why not get a whole pie from the creator herself" He finished with a smirk.

"Oh." momma said flattered while motioning him to stop it.

"I'm serious. It's the best pecan pie north of the Mississippi." Jacob stated. He was not a country boy, but it was cute to see him try to be.

I just rolled my eyes and he looked at me funny. I think my mouth was wide open just watching these two go back and forth with this awkward flirting. Momma put a whole pie in a box and handed it to him.

"Here you go J.T. On the house." she said.

"Seriously?" he asked happily. "That is mighty sweet of you Misses H."

Then he winked at her, smiled at me, and turned around to leave. She took a deep sigh and said all flustered,

"phew, if I wasn't 40 years younger. mmm."

"Eww!", I thought to myself. After momma walked away, I texted Jacob and said, "What in the world was that?" He stopped just outside the door, pulled his phone from his back pocket and turned around after he saw my message. He winked at me too then continued on his way. As he was leaving, Laura Lynn was coming in. Her jaw hit the floor and just stared at him walking away. She rushed up to me and said excitedly, "Oh My God, was that our Hobnobs eye candy?"

"Yup." I replied.

"Did you talk to him? Did you get his name? Oh my god, you went for it. You totally went for it." She blurted out.

"What? No." I declared. "He's actually my new neighbors' son and is friends with Braydon."

"Oh dang. He is young." she responded. "Oh well, he's still nice to look at."

"So, what can I do for you?" I asked her. Then out of the corner of my eye I saw Jacob walking slowly by the window. Then again going the opposite direction. He did that a couple times, each time looking at me with a suspicious grin. 'What is he up to?', I thought. Only seconds passed when a delivery truck stops in front of the shop and the driver gets out carrying a large, gorgeous bouquet of sunflowers, daisies, and black eyed Susans.

"Flowers for Elizabeth Harper." he said as he handed them to me.

Laura Lynn's jaw dropped again. I read the note that came with them and it said, "Your secret admirer."

"Are those from...?" she started to say while pointing her thumb back at the door insinuating they were from Jacob.

"Now why on earth would they be from him?" I replied.

I turned behind me to put them on the counter and when I spun back around, Jacob was outside the window covering his mouth as to say "oops". I stared at him frustrated and Laura Lynn turned around. But he was already gone.

"Something's going on with you. And I'm gonna find out." she said with a playful attitude.

She finished her order and I wrapped it up for her to go. After she left, I took out my phone to text Jacob. "Are you out of your flipping mind? You are crazy." I wrote. He texted back "Crazy for you." and I responded with a rolling eye emoji. 'Could that line be any more cheesy and unoriginal?' I thought. I finished my day at the shop and headed home. When I walked in the front door, I got a text message from him with one word, "Dinner?". I quickly said "No" and closed my phone.

It was a chill night. We just played cards and watched some tv. It was kind of nice to just relax with the kids. The next day after I arrived at the shop, he sends me another one-word text. "Lunch?" And again, I quickly responded, "No." He just doesn't give up does he? I've been trying really hard not to think about him and just let him be Braydon's friend, but he makes it so challenging. It took every fiber in my being not to actively think about him. I have to hum a song or listen to music, but even then, something reminds me of him. If I don't dismiss the very thought of him the instant it enters my mind, I'm going to give in to him. And I can't have that.

After dinner that night, I decided to take the kids for ice cream. Braydon was home for the night and Bella had been asking me for some all week. We went to Miller's Ice Cream house down on Main St. We said hello to Mr. Miller, not Mr. Miller the senior, but his son Anthony. We got our order and sat down at one of the tables closest to the door. No sooner had we started shoving our faces with rocky road and mint chocolate chip, the last person on earth I wanted to see walked through the door. We met eyes but I quickly looked away.

"J.T. What's up?" Braydon said as he stood and went over to shake his hand.

"Hey man. Little miss Bella." he said while smiling at her and Bella giggled. "Miss Harper."

I gave him a quick glance and continued eating my ice cream.

"So, what you got going on tonight?" Braydon asked.

"Uh, nothing." J.T. replied.

"Want to come hang out at my house?" Braydon asked and I started choking on my ice cream.

"Are you ok mom?" Bella asked.

"Mmhmm." I answered while clearing my throat. "Don't you have a project due Braydon? We were gonna work on it."

"Oh crap. That's right." Braydon responded.

"Well, I can help you work on it." Jacob chimed in.

I gave him the stink eye as Braydon asked, "Really? That's awesome man. Is that ok with you mom?"

"Uh, no, that's not a good idea." I said a little annoyed.

"Wait. What? Why?" Braydon asked.

"Cause I know you." I replied. "You'll easily get distracted. Not tonight. But it was a kind gesture. Thank you."

"Uh, fine." Braydon replied with an irritated tone.

"Hey, man. It's cool." Jacob said as he looked at me kind of heart broken. "I'll see you around."

He walked away and went to the counter and started talking to Anthony. He turned around and looked at me and I just turned away. This is why it's just so damn hard to forget about him. He's everywhere. He'll always be everywhere. This is a small town. And I just got here. I ain't leaving. That night we spent the evening working on Braydon's project.

The next morning, Jacob sends me yet another one-word text, "Coffee?" I didn't even reply this time and I tried to avoid any message he sent from that moment on. Braydon was spending most of his free time with Jacob and I just wanted them to be friends. I didn't want to get in the way of that. Besides, it gave me more time to spend with Bella. She's never had a dad in her life. Not a good one at least. I'm all she's got. And I wanted her to feel loved because she most certainly is. We would play dolls and watch movies. We'd make popcorn and have fights with it. It was like having a permanent sleep over.

One Tuesday night, I was sitting at the table going over a cake order for the following week. Bella was watching tv and Braydon was on the couch looking through his phone. Then, momma came around the corner dressed in a beautiful sparkly dress with makeup on and her hair done up nice.

"Momma!" I said amazed.

"Grandma, you look fantastic." Bella said with her eyes opened wide.

"Where are you going?" I asked.

"You won't believe this, but I ran in to Malcolm Miller at IGA's and we got to talking about the Concords and the old house." She said. "Turns out he likes bridge. So, we're heading to the community center to play a few games tonight."

"So, like, a date?" I said with a smile.

"It might be." momma replied flirtatiously.

"Well then, you go and have some much-needed fun, momma." I said as I gave her a hug.

"But not too much fun." Braydon said jokingly out of nowhere.

Me and momma had our mouths wide open from that comment but then we laughed. She went out the front door and I turned to the kids and said, "Well. What should we do for dinner?"

Bella yelled out, "Pizza!"

"That sounds good to me." Braydon responded.

"If I order, will you go pick it up?" I asked him. "You can take my car."

He got super excited and said, "Deal!"

"Can I come?" Bella asked.

"And you have to take your sister." I added.

He rolled his eyes and said "Fine" than I made a call to Big Woods to order. About 20 minutes go by and I tell Bray to go on and head out to pick up the food. He leaves with Bella, I shout "Be careful" and they left. It seems like only seconds after they leave, the doorbell rings. Puzzled, I go to answer it wondering who it could be. When I opened it, there stood Jacob, out of breath with a face of uncertainty.

"Jacob." I exclaimed with nervousness taking over me. "What are you doing here?"

"I needed to see you." he said while breathing heavily. I just stood there staring at him not knowing what I should do.

"Can I please come in?" He asked. "I just wanna talk. Just for a sec"

"Just for a sec." I told him cause the kids would be back any moment.

He walked in the door and I looked outside to make sure no one was around. I closed the door and followed him to the kitchen. I leaned against the wall by the sink and his back was facing me.

"What do you want?" I asked.

He turned around and replied, "Why have you been avoiding me?"

I didn't answer. "It is driving me crazy that I don't hear from you every day." he continued as he stepped closer to me. "You won't return my texts. You won't call me back. You won't talk to me when I see you in public." He said and each time he spoke he stepped closer and closer to me. I was frozen. Just like I was when I first met him. And every time he got closer, my heart would beat faster and faster.

"I know you think I'm too young. But I also know I can make you happy." He expressed then he put his hand against the wall behind me with his arm alongside my face. "And when I'm with you, I'm happy."

My breathing escalated from normal to heavy in seconds. My heart was beating in my throat. His lips were inching closer and closer to mine then he whispered to me while our lips were almost touching, "Let me make you happy Elizabeth Harper." Just when he was about to kiss me, the front door was unlocking. I pushed him away and walked fast out of the kitchen. Braydon came in with Bella following and looked at me strange. Then he looked at Jacob and his face shifted from odd to concerned.

"J.T.?" Braydon began. "What are you doing here?"

"I was coming to see you bro." Jacob replied hesitantly.

Braydon's face turned to relief and asked, "Oh. You wanna stay for some pizza?"

"No," I spoke up as I turned around. They both looked at me then I continued. "I really just want to spend some time with my kids if that's ok."

Jacob seemed disappointed and so did Bray.

"I'll come over after, ok?" Bray said to Jacob.

Jacob looked at me blushing from embarrassment, nodded and left to go home. While the kids and I were eating, my body was there but my mind wasn't. I was doing the motions, but I kept replaying what just happened over and over in my mind. It was exhilarating. It's been so long since I've felt this way for someone. I kept wishing I could see where this could go with Jacob. But I just can't.

"Mom." Braydon said. And I heard him but was still in my own head. "MOM!" He said louder.

I looked at him puzzled then he asked, "Are you ok?"

"Yes." I responded. "Why?"

"You just seem distant." Braydon replied.

"I'm ok. I promise."

After we ate and I cleaned off the table, Braydon said he was going to head to J.T.'s. At first, I was acting like I didn't want him to go. But he pleaded his case of how awesome it felt to have a friend again. So, I gave in. As Bella and I watch tv, I found myself yet again dazed and in my own little world. I was flipping my phone up and down debating whether I should message him to discuss what just happened. But I'm afraid I'll like what I hear so I set it on the coffee table and just left it there. When it was time to put Bella to bed, I gave her a kiss and closed her door. I sat on the couch and was waiting for Braydon to come home when through the door comes momma.

"Hey." I shouted with curiosity. "How'd it go?"

She sighed and swayed her way over to the couch and just melted into the cushions.

"It was the best night I have had in a very, very long time." She said while grinning from ear to ear.

She proceeded to tell me about all the sweet and funny things her and Mr. Miller would talk about. It was just so nice to see her smiling and happy again. It seemed like everyone in this house was happy but me.

"Did you hear what I said?" momma asked.

"What? No. I'm sorry." I replied somewhat flustered.

She put her hand on my arm and said "Hey, your time will come. Love will find you. I can feel it." She caressed my cheek and we both smiled. She said she was going to head to bed, and I said goodnight. Shortly after, Braydon came home.

"Hey mom." he said to me while walking toward his room.

"You have fun?" I shouted.

"Yup." and he closed his bedroom door behind him. I waited for a few minutes, watching Braydon's door to see if he would come out. Then I quickly got up, grabbed my phone and stepped quietly outside. I started to dial Jacobs number, but I never hit send. I was baffled. Mad. Excited. Anxious. Like it's always a roller coaster of emotions when it comes to Jacob. My leg started bouncing in anticipation. This is ridiculous, I thought. And I finally hit call.

"I was hoping it was you." Jacob answered the phone saying.

"What the hell?" I yelled. "Stop doing this."

"Doing what?" he answered. "Stop liking you? Stop thinking about you? Cause I can't do that."

"Yes, you can. I've had to do it and I'm doing just fine." I replied.

Then there was silence for a minute.

"Jacob?" I asked. "Jacob? Are you there?"

"You had to stop thinking about me?" He asked quietly.

Crap. Then I was the one silent. And I was tongue tied.

"I ... I have to go." I said and hung up the phone.

I grunted with annoyance then walked back inside. I paced the living room a bit desperately trying not to think about our close encounter, our lips barely touching, how he smelled so good. I shook my head and thought to myself, 'Get out of my head!'. This isn't good. Things just got way worse. What am I going to do?

The next day I woke up feeling a little sad. I wasn't really sure why. But I just moped around the house, the shop, the store. Everywhere I went I swear I saw Jacob. But it was just my mind playing tricks on me. I'm fortunate to have a job working at the bakery though. It has been really nice to work alongside momma. She makes some delicious desserts. But her and Mr. Miller seem to be dating now. Which is a little weird because he's not my dad. And I know he wouldn't want momma to live out the rest of her days alone. But it's still a little strange. I like Mr. Miller a lot and I'm extremely happy for momma. I haven't seen her smile like that since daddy was around. But at the same time, it just reminded me how much I was alone. Mr. Miller started coming to the bakery every day on his lunch break to bring her a single red rose that he picked from his garden. I couldn't help but smile. But I also was a little jealous. I could just imagine Jacob being that way. "Stop it." I told myself, and continued working.

That night at dinner, I was just pushing my food around on the plate. I didn't want to eat. I just kept thinking about how everyone was happy, but I was not.

"You ok Beth?" momma asked concerned.

I lifted my head up and replied, "I need to get out of the house. Is that ok?"

She nodded her head 'yes' and I excused myself from the table. I got in my car and texted Peggy Sue, asking her if I could come over. She said that would be fine and texted me her address. On the way there, Jacob texted me. 'You doing ok?' But I didn't reply. It's like he's watching me and knows when I leave or when I'm home alone. It's a little weird and flattering at the same time. When I got to Peggy's house, I knocked on the door and Billy Joe answered.

"Hey." I said. "I'm sorry to barge in like this."

"No, its fine. Come on in." Billy Joe said.

I followed him to the living room which was buried in toys for kids of all ages. There was Peggy Sue sitting on the couch nursing little Elizabeth.

"Hey there." She said. "Come sit."

"Thanks for letting me come over." I stated.

"It's no problem at all. You ok?"

The second she asked that, I just started crying. She moved the baby and fixed her shirt then asked Billy Joe to take the baby and kids to give them some privacy. He complied and left the room telling the little ones to "Come on."

"What's going on?" She asked as she took my hands and looked concerned.

I took a deep breath and began to tell her how I was feeling. She was shocked when I told her about momma and Mr. Miller. She was happy for

Braydon and Bella making friends but could understand why I felt so lonely. She just listened and let me vent.

"I'm so sorry you have to deal with this sugar." She began. "But you don't have to be alone you know?"

"What do you mean?" I asked.

"Laura Lynn told me about the flowers you got."

I tried to act like I didn't know anything about them.

"You can tell me. I won't judge." She said. "Hell, if I wasn't married to that big ole loof I'd be asking that eye candy to give me some sugar."

I softly laughed then I said, "There's nothing to tell. He's Braydon's friend. And he's 20 years old. Bray is finally smiling again. I couldn't do that to him."

"Braydon's almost a man." she said, "and you're only human."

What she said made sense. I am a grown woman and can make my own decisions. But why does this one seem so wrong?

"There's really nothing." I told her.

"Suit yourself." she replied with a smile.

I stayed for a few minutes more then was on my way out. I didn't want to go home right away so I went for a drive. I started to wonder what Jacob was doing at this very moment. I wondered if he was at our spot, thinking about things like I would be doing right now if I was there. In fact, I think that's where I'll go. The whole ride down to the lake the silence was so loud. I decided to make a deal with myself. If he was there, I would give him and I a chance. But there had to be some rules. For starters, we couldn't tell anyone. Everything we did had to be in secret. If he's not there, I'll leave him alone for good and move on from the thought of us. I turned down the dirt road that led to my rock hoping he was there yet wishing he wasn't. But low and behold, there was his truck, parked all alone by the trees. I turned off my headlights and parked my car to begin the short hike to the shoreline. I came around the bend and there he was, sitting on the rock and peering into the water.

"I was hoping I'd find you here." I said as I startled him.

He turned around and replied, "Jesus, you scared me."

I walked over to him and propped myself on the rock next to him. I looked at the moon that was reflecting on the water before I turned to him and said, "So...should we really do this?"

He looked at me and asked, "Do what?"

I could see his heart beating faster in the vein of his neck after I responded with, "Us."

He looked at me for a moment, his eyes beaming with warmth and passion. Then what he asked next completely threw me off guard.

"Come with me to Washington." He stated with all seriousness.

"What?" I declared confused.

He looked back out towards the water and continued. "I got an invitation for Amanda and Jeremys wedding."

He told me then turned to look back at me. "I don't want to do this alone. Come with me."

Once again, I found myself speechless. I was silent for a few seconds then Jacob said as he grabbed my hand, "Elizabeth? Please. I CAN'T do this alone."

How was I going to do this? I would have to lie to my family. I would have to make up some story as to where I was going and why. I took a deep breath, sighed with anxiety then answered him saying, "Ok. I'll go". His face lit up and he looked so happy. And for the first real time since I've been here, so was I. He put his arm around me and I just laid my head on his shoulder. He talked about getting separate hotel rooms because you know, he was a gentleman like that. He said he would take care of all the arrangements. He would even pay for everything. He just wanted to spend time with me, with no distractions, no chances of anyone seeing us, just us. This was crazy. This was absolutely nuts! I can't believe I agreed to do this. Part of me wanted to back out, to tell him he was out of his damn mind, to just walk away. But the other part of me was so much stronger. The urge to be near him and spend every second with him was so appealing. And now that this is actually going to happen, I have to figure out a story that everyone will believe.

Chapter 7

The next few weeks were kind of a blur leading up to the Washington trip. I told Braydon, Bella and momma that I was going back to Colorado to take care of some lose ends regarding the kids and annoying court stuff. Jacob told his family he was going to the wedding, obviously. And ironically, Braydon was going to New York for his senior trip the same week. He would be flying out Monday and we were flying out Friday morning. The wedding was the same night. We were only making it a weekend trip, but I was extremely excited. We met at the airport at 8:30 a.m. and walked to our gate together. We got checked in and started boarding the plane. This is it, I thought to myself. No going back now.

"I can't believe this is happening." Jacob said a few minutes after we sat in our seats.

"I know, right? It's crazy." I replied.

We talked most of the 5-hour flight. At one point, we shared headphones as we watched the tv show FRIENDS which we both absolutely loved. It was kind of funny when the flight attendant came up to us. She asked Jacob if him and his wife would like a beverage.

"Oh, we're not married." I said.

"Yet." he replied then looked at me raising his eyebrows. I nudged him in the arm and said "Stop."

He snickered and continued watching the show. Once we landed and got our luggage, he haled for a taxi to get to our hotel. I had no idea where we were staying or anything about Seattle. I had never been here before. The only thing I knew was this is where they filmed the movie "Sleepless In Seattle" and I mentioned that to Jacob.

"It's actually not too far from where we're staying." He said.

"Really?" I asked.

And no sooner had I asked that, we pulled up to this beautiful hotel called the Charter Hotel right inside the city. We walked into the lobby and I just looked around in awe at how beautiful everything was. And in all the years I was married to both Mitch and Jefferey, they never took me to places like this. Not even for our anniversary. We never even ate at nice restaurants before.

"Jacob." I said astounded. "This place is beautiful!"

"I was hoping you'd like it." He responded with a smile.

We went to the front desk and asked to check in.

"Oh. There must be a mistake Mr. and Mrs. Brooks. I see we accidently booked and charged you for 2 rooms." the receptionist stated.

"Oh, no. It's not a mistake." I responded. "We each have our own room."

"That's right." he added while rolling his eyes. "We're not married."

"Oh, ok." she replied. "Then let me get those keys for you."

As we waited, I looked around and saw the sign for Amanda and Jeremy's wedding. It was at 6pm in this very hotel.

"Here you go. We hope you enjoy your stay." the lady at the front desk said as she handed us our card keys.

We got in the elevator and headed to the 4th floor. We walked down the hall and he stopped at room 402.

"This is me." he said.

I walked past him to room 403. "And I'm here." I responded.

We both smiled then he said, "Pick you up in an hour."

We went into our rooms and immediately I was drawn to the view of the city outside the window. I rolled my bag in and set it next to the tv. I just looked around and took it all in. Just then, the phone in my room rang. I picked it up wondering who it could be.

"Hello?" I said with a perplexed tone.

"This is room service." said Jacob on the other end. "Would you be needing anything else this evening madam?"

I laughed and said in my best British accent "No sir. My room is superb."

He giggled and said "Excellent. Your escort will accompany you at 5:30 this evening."

"Thank you." I responded.

There was a pause for a moment, then Jacob replied in the sweetest tone, "No, thank you for coming."

We hung up the phone and I went to draw a bath. The bathroom had complimentary bubble bath, soaps and a towel that looked like a swan sitting on the sink counter. I was enjoying every second of my bubble bath. Once I was done, I put on the robe provided by the hotel and started doing my makeup. I curled my hair, put on lipstick then went to put on my dress. It was red, form fitting, just to my knee and had small cap sleeves with a sweetheart neckline. It ruched in the center and had a line of red sequins going across in a diagonal line. I put on my earrings, a necklace and a bracelet to match. I sprayed a little perfume on each side of my neck and saw myself in the mirror. Damn, I looked good! As I was putting on my red satin heels and just about to buckle the last strap, there was a knock at the door. I opened it and there stood Jacob, all suave and debonair in his black suit and red tie.

"You look...." he paused and just eyed me up and down. Then he finished by saying, "...you look absolutely stunning."

"Thank you." I said while blushing. "So do you."

We both just got lost in each other's eyes and then I realized I forgot to give him a gift I had got him.

"Oh, I almost forgot." I said as I went back into the room and grabbed the small white box with a black ribbon.

"What's this?" Jacob asked after I handed him the box.

"Just a little something I picked up for you." I responded.

He looked at me like a lost puppy dog and said, "That is so sweet."

"Open it." I exclaimed.

He opened the box and inside was a tie clip shaped like a guitar pick. I saw it one day when I walked in to the Men's Toy Shop as I was trying to find a graduation gift for Braydon. The second I saw it I immediately thought of Jacob.

"What?" He said surprised and excited.

"Do you like it?" I asked as I watched him put it in on his tie.

"I love it." He said with a smile than he leaned over and kissed my cheek.

He put out his arm to escort me and I slowly put my hand in it. We walked down the hallway to the elevator and the whole time he just kept looking at me and smiling. We got into the elevator and he couldn't stop staring at me.

"What?" I asked.

"I can't believe I'm here with you right now." He said.

I smirked and responded, "Neither can I."

We walked onto the rooftop where the ceremony was going to take place. It was beautiful, adorned with stringed lights and black sheer panels of fabric wrapped in a spiral around the pillars. Alongside the glass wall on the edge of the rooftop were dozens of bouquets of red roses. You could see the whole city from up here.

"That is Elliot Bay." Jacob said as he pointed to the body of water in the distance.

The chairs were black, and everything looked modern and elegant. We took our seats and no sooner had we sat down, a voice from behind yells, "Jacob Brooks." We both turned around to see this short caucasian guy with a beard and mustache yet no hair on his head. He was dressed in a tuxedo with a red tie and cumber bun.

"Seth Fisher." Jacob said as he stood up to give him a bro handshake and hug.

"How's it going man?" he asked. Then he noticed me stand up next to Jacob and continued, "Must be going good."

"Seth Fisher, this is Elizabeth Harper." Jacob introduced us.

"Nice to meet you." I replied.

"Likewise." said Seth as we shook hands.

They started talking about how he and I met, and I asked how he knew Jacob. Apparently, Seth, Jacob, the bride Amanda and the groom Jeremy all grew up in high school together and went to the same college. But when everything went down, I guess Jacob learned pretty quickly that Seth was closer to the groom. Once Seth left the conversation Jacob turned around and just looked out to the city and sat down.

"You ok?" I asked as I sat down too.

"Yea, I'm fine." he said trying to play it off even though I knew he wasn't.

The ceremony began and everything seemed to go smoothly, I have to admit. But Jacob was a little quieter than usual. I can't imagine what he must be feeling. So, during the vows, I reached over and held his hand. He looked at me and smiled then let out a deep sigh. After the ceremony, we entered into the reception hall and found Jacob's name and guest card on the table that said table #8. He only knew one person at our table and that was Amanda's older cousin Dwayne, who was a little bit odd. We ate our dinner without talking a whole lot. I tried to get him to tell me what was on his mind, but he kept assuring me he was fine. Later, the bride and groom were starting to make their rounds thanking everyone at each table. Jacobs' legs started to bounce in agitation knowing they would be coming to our table soon.

"Hey," I said softly as I put my hand on his leg. "It's gonna be ok."

"I'm so happy you're here." He responded.

"There he is, Jacob Brooks himself." said a voice behind us. We turned to look to see the bride and groom who both had very awkward expressions on their faces, which was to be expected.

"Hi J." Amanda said.

"Hey." he responded.

"We're glad you could make it." Amanda continued.

"Yes, it was big of you to come man." Jeremy said.

But Jacob didn't say anything. You could literally cut the tension with a knife.

"And are you like his aunt or something?" Amanda asked.

How dare she call me his aunt.

"Guys, this is..." Jacob started but I quickly cut him off and answered saying, "I'm his wife."

All of them, including Jacob looked surprised. But he quickly smiled and put his arm around me and agreed.

"Oh" Amanda stumbled. "Congratulations."

"Yes, Congratulations." Jeremy said stunned and put his arm around Amanda's waist. "We really should move on. Got a lot of thank-you's to say."

They both walked away with very fake smiles on their faces. Then me and Jacob started to laugh.

"Thank you" he said with a grin.

"Ugh, your aunt?" I said. "Figured everyone else thought I was your wife so why not them too?"

We had a good chuckle and both of us took a swig of our drinks that were on the table. Then one of my favorite songs of all time started playing from the DJ's speakers. Jacob stood up, held out his hand and said, "Care to dance Mrs. Brooks?"

I smiled and said, "But of course Mr. Brooks." and placed my hand in his.

He led me to the dance floor and put his right arm around my waist ever so gently. He held my right hand with his left hand close to his heart and pulled me in close. We started to dance and I was again impressed that this man had excellent rhythm.

"Where did you learn to dance?" I asked.

"My grandma taught me." He replied. "She told me that a gentleman must do more than just pull-out chairs and open car doors. A true gentleman must learn everything he needs to learn in order to make his woman happy."

"Your grandma is a smart woman." I responded with a smile.

"Was." He said. "She was a great woman."

"I'm sorry." I stated

"No, it's fine." he said stopping me. "She died when I was 12. I do miss her though. You would have loved her."

He pulled me closer and rested his cheek alongside mine and said, "You smell fantastic."

Then he started to softly sing the words to the song that was playing which was Tennessee

Whiskey by Chris Stapelton. But before he could sing the last line of the chorus, I moved my head to look directly into his eyes. My heart started beating out of my chest and I felt that his did too. Our breathing got heavy and he slowly leaned in. I began to close my eyes and his lips were almost completely touching mine when he paused. I opened my eyes and he just held his lips there for a few seconds. And then, he finally kissed me. This may sound like something out of a cheesy fairy tale movie but it felt like the whole room was spinning. Everything was a blur. And our bodies were floating in midair. We kissed until the song ended and then we both just stared at each other, breathing heavy and didn't move from the dance floor. A fast song came on and everyone around us started dancing. But we just stood there while everything around us was hazy. He smiled at me and that was it. I was no longer going to hold back.

"Get your coat." I said into his ear.

He quickly nodded his head 'yes' and bolted to the table to get our things as I waited by the exit. He came back and grabbed my hand and with haste went towards the elevator. We were the only ones waiting to go down, everyone else was still enjoying the reception. So, when we got in the elevator and Jacob pushed the button to our floor, we knew we were alone. The doors had barely shut all the way when he just took me in his arms and kissed me. He kissed me all the way down to the 4th floor. He kept passionately kissing me all the way to his room. He fumbled for the key while taking off his tie still kissing me the whole time. We went into his room, and we both kicked off our shoes and kept kissing. And well? I'm a lady. I'm not going to tell you all the passionate details, but I will say this....it was the absolute most amazing night of my entire life. No one has ever touched me the way he does or kissed me the way he has or even looked at me the way he does. He literally takes my breath away. And there was definitely no going back now. I was his and he was mine. I was committed to doing the same thing for him as he said he would do for me, make him happy. As long as it was in secret, of course.

A couple hours later and we were just lying there under the covers. My head was on his chest and he was rubbing my shoulder. We didn't have to say anything. Just lying there next to him skin to skin was perfect. But then my curious mind got the best of me. I sat up, rested my chin on my hand that was on his chest and just looked at him smiling.

"So, how long were you and Amanda together?" I asked.

"Are you serious?" He said nervously laughing. "We just made love and you want to talk about my ex?"

"Did you just say, 'made love'?" I questioned.

"Oh my god." He responded while rubbing his eyes.

"Come on. Just tell me." I said.

He sighed and started telling me the story of how they met in high school. Him and Jeremy had been friends since 2nd grade and when they started freshman year there was this girl who caught every guy's attention. Jeremy, Seth and the other guys around made a bet with Jacob that he couldn't get Amanda to even notice him. But he said he boldly went up to her, introduced himself and asked her out on a date right off the bat. She said 'yes' and the rest was history. They dated all through high school and he proposed at graduation. But when they got to college things seemed strange. 6 months later, he catches her and Jeremy in her dorm room. I felt so bad for him. He didn't deserve that and she definitely didn't deserve him. We talked all through the night about his life and our pasts. I told him about Mitch and me as well as my situation with Jefferey. He seemed to really listen. And he seemed to understand. And yet, I still couldn't believe that this amazing young guy chose me. He was sweet and funny, thoughtful and romantic. The fact that he was 20 seemed to dissipate from my mind the more I was with him. We fell asleep in each other's arms which has never happened to me before either. And I was loving every second.

The next morning, I woke up and realized Jacob wasn't there. I called his name but no answer. I sat up and was shocked to see all of my things from my room neatly folded and organized now in his room. I called his name again while looking around the room and still, no Jacob. When I propped myself up, my hand felt paper underneath the sheets. It was a note that said, 'Get dressed. Wear something comfortable and meet me in the lounge.' I smiled as I noticed he signed his name with an xoxo. I quickly got up, put on some comfy clothes, and rushed out the door to see him. When I exited the elevator and headed to the lounge, I caught sight of him sitting at a table with a single rose in a vase next to 2 coffee cups. He stood up and smiled. I went over to him and embraced him tightly.

"I hope you don't mind but I took the liberty of ordering you breakfast." He said as he took the carafe of coffee and poured it into my cup.

"Well, that all depends. What did you order?" I said in a playful manner.

"Pancakes covered in strawberries with a side of bacon. " He replied.

I was shocked. I told him that was my favorite breakfast since I was a kid the first time we ever talked in his truck driving to the lake. My parents would wake me up every Sunday morning with pancakes smothered in sautéed strawberries and a side of bacon. I would always dip my bacon in the syrup that I had poured all over the pancakes. It was so good. Moments later, the waiter came out and set down in front of me a delicious looking portion of pancakes topped with strawberries and a side of bacon. I looked at Jacob and smiled.

"You're amazing." I told him.

"Because of you." He replied.

I then started to dig into this fabulous breakfast. Everything tasted so delightful. And the company was even better. I couldn't believe I was sitting across from this gorgeous, generous man with a fantastic view overlooking the city.

"So." I started. "What are we doing today?"

"I thought I'd give you a tour of my city." He responded with a smile.

After breakfast, we took a taxi over to Lake Union where they filmed Sleepless in Seattle. We also walked through Pike Place Market and Alki Beach where we tried to reenact the scene with Noah and his dad. I'm a bit bigger than Noah so we sort of fell into the sand. We laughed and he kissed me while I was laying down on the beach. We took the Ferry over to Explorer Trail and walked along the paths that went through the trees. He kissed me every moment he could. It was romantic. It's like he can't get enough of me. We had lunch at this little place called Boat Shed Restaurant that was right on the water under Manette Bridge. We drove through this neighborhood and he showed me the house where he grew up. It was right next to Bainbridge Highschool that he and his friends attended. We took a Taxi later that day back to downtown and began walking down 2nd Avenue where we entered into the Seattle Art Museum. We admired all the local art on display and tried to make poses to match what was on some of the canvases. We kept walking and checking out all the buildings and sights there was to see. It was a busy city. We then headed to the big Ferris wheel just before dark and watched the sunset from 175 feet in the air. We walked hand in hand wherever we went.

As we strolled down Cherry Street, we came to a place called Twilight Exit. There was a sign outside the front entrance that read "Karaoke Tonight" underneath the list of drink specials.

"Come on." he said as he smiled and led me inside.

It was an eclectic little place with red and yellow lantern lights hanging from the ceiling. It had a mural of a sunset which almost resembled the one we just saw. There were trophies on the shelves from the local football team. And a few arcade machines in the back towards the restrooms. We found a little round table in the center by the bar and we could hear a woman singing who was standing on a small stage next to the karaoke DJ.

"I'll be right back." He said to me as I was sitting down.

He walked over to the DJ and asked him something, probably about a song, and the DJ shook his head 'yes'. He came back to his seat with a huge grin on his face.

"What are you up to?" I asked with suspicion.

"Oh, you'll see." he answered with a mischievous smirk.

The waitress came and asked what we wanted to drink. I ordered my favorite drink which was a Long Island Iced Tea. Jacob ordered a sweet tea and said, "Designated driver." Which obviously wasn't true considering we walked there. But him being 20 and all makes ordering an alcoholic beverage a little challenging. After our drinks arrived and I took my first sip, the DJ called Jacob's name to the stage. I watched him walk up wondering what song he was going to dazzle me with that evening.

"This one's for the beautiful girl in the blue dress sitting right there." he said into the mic while pointing at me.

I shook my head and just smiled at him while those around me looked at me and smiled as well. The music started playing and I could see people in the audience slowly bobbing their heads along to the beat. Then he opened his mouth to sing the song Make It Easy by Jason Aldean. This man has an amazing voice. The crowd started cheering and hollering, clapping their hands and smiling at me. He got off the stage and started walking around the room while singing the next line. He stole some guy's cowboy hat that was sitting close to the stage and just kept singing, not missing a beat.

During the instrumental break, he came up to me and held out his hand to help me up off my seat. He then wrapped his arms around my waist pulling me in super close. He looked me in my eyes, gave me the most alluring smile and said something that I was not expecting.

"I'm falling in love you Elizabeth Harper." and then he kissed me.

The crowd around us went nuts, cheering and hollering as loud as they could. After he kissed me, he leaned his forehead against mine and sang the last line. He gave me another quick kiss and walked back toward the stage singing the last chorus. My brain just flashed back to this entire weekend, how the lyrics pretty much summed up how our trip actually went. We stole kisses under covers, lying in bed all twisted with each other. It's literally like the song was written for me from him. 'Did he just say he loved me?' I thought to myself. I didn't say it back though. I couldn't say it back. This isn't love, is it? It's just a romantic fling, right? Oh god, I hope he wasn't expecting it back.

When he was done singing the song, he walked off the small stage, gave the man back his hat and high-fived people in the audience as he walked back towards his seat. Everyone was clapping and telling him how amazing he did. When he reached our table, he gave me a warm embrace from behind, a kiss on the cheek, and sat down.

"That was amazing." I said to him with a smile.

He just looked at me grinning and drank his sweet iced tea. I can't believe he said he loved me. I was never expecting that. I looked at him somewhat speechless again not knowing how to respond to that. He probably could tell I was a little dumbfounded cause he leaned over and said in my ear ever so softly, "I know you don't feel the same. And that's ok. But I couldn't hold it in any longer."

He looked in my eyes and I just smiled. It's not that I didn't feel anything, I was just stunned that he feels love. I gave him a kiss and said, "You're a wonderful man Jacob Brooks." Then he kissed me right back with a very romantic kiss.

We enjoyed the rest of our night watching people sing and talking like usual. There was always talking. We never ran out of things to say. At one point I did get a little sad knowing this was our last night alone together. I wondered how things would be once we got back to Indiana. How would we be able to spend time together? It is going to be tricky and I do feel guilty for sneaking around. But when I'm with him, I forget about all that. Not sure if it's a good thing or a bad thing. But what I do know is, at this very moment, I'm going to just enjoy every second we have together until the plane lands tomorrow in Indiana.

Chapter 8

It's Sunday morning and we're about to touch down in Indiana. It was a quiet flight, not because we didn't have anything to say, but because we didn't have to say anything. Just being next to him was enough. After the plane landed in Indianapolis and we collected our bags from the conveyor, we walked with our arms around each other out of the airport. We went to his truck first and we kissed for a long time goodbye. After our wonderful kiss, we embraced for a moment, then he asked me, "When does Braydon's flight get in again?"

"3:40" I responded.

He looked at his watch and noticed it was 3:17.

"Ugh, one more." he said as he leaned in to kiss me again. We started to part ways with our hands holding each other's until we were too far apart to touch.

"I'll call you." I said as he backed away toward his truck.

"You better." He replied.

I walked toward my car to put my luggage in the trunk. I kept turning around to see his face and every time I did, he would wave. I finally made it back into the airport to wait for Braydon to get off his flight from his senior trip. I made one last turn around to see Jacob driving out of the parking lot. I sighed to myself and smiled then walked towards Gate 2B. As Braydon and his classmates walked out of the gate exit, he saw me and started to smile.

"Mom." He called out.

"Hey." I responded, "welcome home champ. How was it?"

"It was so much fun." He said giving me a side hug.

The whole ride home he told me all about his trip and how he got to sit next to Sabrina Lanmaster. I assumed he had a crush on her because she was in a lot of his stories.

"Sabrina Lanmaster. I think her family owns a landscaping company."

"Yea, called LandMasters." he said. We both laughed a little at the play on words and thought it was clever.

"So, tell me more about Miss Sabrina. Is she your girlfriend?" I asked.

"MOM." He muttered all embarrassed.

I tried to get him to tell me more, but he was acting all shy. So, she must be someone special cause I've never seen him this worked up over a girl. When we got home, Bella ran up to him and tried to give him a hug. But remember Braydon is not a hugger. Momma came up too and asked how it was. He then started to tell her some of what he told me as I gave Bella a hug. Then momma turned to me and asked, "How did everything go in Colorado?"

"It was fine." I answered.

Just then my phone went off with a text message and I saw that it was Jacob asking if I got home ok. I texted him "Yes" with a winky face and then I put my phone in my pocket. I turned around, looked towards the Miller house and saw him standing by his truck with his phone in his hand looking in my direction. I smiled and so did he. This is where the hiding and lying really starts to take off.

"I think I'm gonna take a shower." I said as walked toward my room.

The entire shower I smiled to myself remembering all the amazing moments Jacob and I had this past weekend. It was surreal. I had only been back home for 2 hours and I already miss him. I already want to see him again. But how? Coming up with excuses and reasons to leave the house is going to be tricky but I'll do whatever it takes.

Over the next few weeks, Jacob and I tried to spend as much time together as we possibly could. We would meet down at his spot or my spot by the lake where we would laugh and talk for hours. There weren't too many places we could go for fear of being seen. And every time Braydon had him over, he'd always walk by me, smile and say. "Hello Miss. Harper." then wink as he passed by. I have to admit it was exhilarating having to sneak around. It became easier and easier to do which isn't actually a good thing I've concluded. We would text each other any chance that we could. And talk on the phone when we were driving in our cars by ourselves. For being only 20, he sure is mature and has an amazing personality. He would leave little notes on my car by hiding them under the door handle. Or he would stick them on the outside of my bedroom window so in the morning when I'd wake up to draw back the curtains, I would see it. One time, he left a note on the bathroom mirror that said, "Hello gorgeous" and could only be seen after a hot shower. He was quite the romantic. And his 21st birthday was coming up soon. So, I had to figure out how to do something romantic for him.

One Tuesday afternoon, when I was strolling down Main Street after I was done working at the shop, I ran into Peggy. She was pushing a stroller with baby Elizabeth sleeping in the carrier. I haven't seen her much since I've been back in town. I guess I've been so preoccupied with Jacob that I haven't focused much on anything else.

"Hey there." she said with exhaustion in her voice.

"Hi." I replied. "How are you?"

"I'm good." She replied. "Just tired."

"I can imagine." I said.

She looked at me for a few seconds and continued,

"I've actually been meaning to call you. Do you have some time? Maybe we can go sit and talk somewhere?" she asked.

"Of course." I answered as we started walking together to find a spot.

We walked over to 2 benches that were situated on the sidewalk at the corner of S. Van

Buren and Main. I sat on one bench and she sat on the other then parked Elizabeth's stroller right beside her. She didn't say anything right away. She just sat there staring.

"Is everything ok?" I asked.

She took a deep breath then said, "I saw you." I wasn't quite sure what she meant.

"I saw you and Mr. Eye candy at the airport."

My jaw fell to the floor. I was in disbelief especially since he and I have been so careful.

"We were at the airport picking up Bobby Flyn from his class field trip and I saw you guys walking arm and arm toward the exit." she continued. "I had to distract Billy Joe from seeing you cause I knew he'd say something."

I still wasn't sure what to say. I just sat there confused and scared.

"If somethings going on, you can tell me. In fact, I might high five you cause damn girl, you go." she said and snickered

"Peggy, I..." I began then paused trying to collect my thoughts.

"... but you don't want anyone to know, do you?" she asked.

I shook my head 'no' and almost started to cry. Then she put her hand on my leg and said, "Hey, it's ok. I won't tell anyone. I haven't breathed a word these past couple weeks. But just know, that secrets always come out eventually. Just be careful is all."

This time I shook my head 'yes' and wiped a tear from my cheek. We stood up, hugged and went our separate ways. As I walked to my car, I felt awful. Peggy saw us at the airport. What are the odds? What if someone else sees us? What if they talk? What if Braydon finds out? This could be really bad. I pulled out my phone and texted Jacob saying,

"Hey. We need to talk. Can we meet?" He instantly called me and asked with panic in his voice, "Hey. You ok?"

"I don't know." I replied starting to cry. "I just saw Peggy Sue. She saw us at the airport."

"What? How?" he asked frantic.

"Picking up her son from a school field trip."

"And she's just now telling you?"

"She said she wasn't sure how to talk to me about it cause to her it's not a big deal. But she's known for a while, I think. The last time we talked she questioned things."

"Can you trust her? Do you think she'll say anything?" Jacob asked.

"Yes, I trust her." I answered. "But I'm scared. What if someone else sees and aren't as willing to keep it to themselves?"

"We just have to be more careful." He said. "It'll be ok. I promise"

Jacob had a way of calming me down. I was so worried after Peggy and I spoke. But as soon as I talk to him, every anxiety I have melts away.

"Hey," he said softly. "No matter what happens, I'm not going anywhere. I just wish there were more things we could do together in public without raising suspicion"

I smiled and gained my composure. Then I had a thought. "Do you think you can help me with something?" I asked.

"Anything." he replied.

"I was going to go to the car lot this Saturday and pick out a car for Braydon. It's going to be his graduation present. Do you think when you guys hang out together tonight you can figure out what kind of car he wants?" I asked.

"Absolutely." he responded.

"And will you go with me to pick it out?"

"Like you have to ask." He said.

"Great. That'll give me an excuse to see you and be with you in public." I responded.

"Do you really need an excuse to see me?" He asked giggling.

"No." I replied.

We talked for a little bit more, then I got in to my car and drove to pick up Bella from school. She told me about her day and how some boy was picking on her.

"What? That's terrible." I responded.

"It's ok mom." she said. "Mrs. Jenkins says when a boy picks on you that means he likes you. And Tommy Jenkins is as fine as heck!"

"Well, " I started, " the truth is, if a boy really likes you then he'll be nice to you. I think adults just say that to kids cause they don't want your feelings hurt."

She thought for a second and then responded with her sweet, innocent voice, "Oh, well I have several boys who are nice to me."

I snickered as I looked back at her with a shocked face. We started singing the song that was playing on the radio until we pulled into our driveway. We saw Braydon outside talking to someone who was standing on a ladder. As I got closer, I saw that it was Jacob. He was helping Braydon install a basketball hoop above the garage.

"Hey." I said as I got out of the car. Jacob started coming down the ladder and walked over to us with Braydon. Bella ran to Jacob yelling his name and he got down to her level to give her a hug. He asked her how was school and she was telling him what happened. Then he said to her, "That reminds me. I have something for you."

He then pulled out an old phone and said she could have it.

"It doesn't have service, but you can use it with Wi-Fi. See?" He said as he showed her. "I already put my number in there. That way, if anyone messes with you again, you call me."

Her face lit up and she wrapped her little arms around his neck thanking him. Then Braydon chimed in also to say that he'd 'kick any little boys' ass who messed with his little sister.'

"Watch your mouth." I said as I pointed at him.

He rolled his eyes then Jacob stood up and said to me, "Hello Miss Harper."

"Please. Call me Beth." I replied with a smile.

He smiled back and I started walking toward the house. I put down my things and strolled over to the kitchen sink where I could see out the window with a perfect view of Jacob using hand tools. I just sighed and smiled at this fantastic man who adores me and my kids. And they adore him. I started to question things to myself, wondering if I should just tell everyone, if maybe this could work.

"Whatcha lookin' at?" Momma said as she came into the room and startled me.

"Geez." I said as I put my hand to my chest. "Um, just watching Braydon and Jacob getting along."

"You mean J.T.?" Momma asked.

"Yea, well, it stands for Jacob Tyler." I said. "He told me that the night we were at their house."

"Ah." momma said then she started looking out the window as well.

"It's a shame he's so young." she stated.

"What do you mean a shame?" I asked not sure why she said that.

"Well, he's smart. Charming. Funny. He can cook. He can sing and play an instrument. The kids love him. He has a great job and helps people. Not to mention he's ridiculously handsome."

I chuckled and thought to myself, 'If only you knew, he is all those things and more.'

"He'd be perfect for you. Everything you ever wanted. Too bad he's still a kid." she added. "He'll make a good husband one day to some lucky girl though." She looked at me, smiled then walked away.

Lucky girl? Kid?? Now there's no way for sure I could ever say anything. I can't deal with hurting anyone or disappointing them. I decided to go to my room and put some laundry away. Braydon and Jacob played some basketball for about an hour before we had to eat supper. Jacob went home and I watched him from my bedroom window walk towards his house. After we ate, Bray headed over to Jacobs to hang out. He'd only been gone for about 40 mins when I got a text message from Jacob saying, "Dream car, Lamborghini. For real car, Honda Civic." I laughed to myself then texted back, "Let's see if we can find that Lambo ;-)" then he responded ":-o". I smiled and put my phone down to continue folding clothes. The rest of the night was pretty quiet. We texted a little bit, but Bray was there and I didn't want Jacob to have to keep hiding his phone. I'm sure Braydon would ask who it was.

I'm positive he told Jacob about Sabrina and asked Jacob if he had a girlfriend. Oh gosh, that sounds weird in my head. The thought of my son talking to my secret boyfriend about him and I not knowing it's his mom made me cringe. I just pray Jacob doesn't tell him any details.

Chapter 9

It's Saturday morning and today is the day I get Braydon his first car. I told momma what my plans were for the day and asked her to keep Braydon company. Bella had stayed over at a friend's house last night so I had the next few hours free. After breakfast, Momma asked Braydon if he would help her around back pulling some weeds and fixing part of the fence. He agreed, then I said, "I'm gonna run into town for a bit."

"K." he replied.

I don't suspect he knows a thing about the car. I texted Jacob to see if he was ready and to meet me at the end of the road. I got in my car, went down the street and there he was, dressed in khaki cargo pants, a blue flannel shirt, and black Doc Martens. That shirt really made his gorgeous blue eyes pop even more than they already did. I pulled up to him and rolled down the window.

"Woo sailor! You going my way?" I said putting my sunglasses down and raising my eyebrows.

He smiled and got in the passenger side. He leaned over and kissed my cheek and I told him to be careful cause we didn't want anyone to see.

"I'm sorry." He began. "I just can't help myself when I'm around you."

"Well, try." I said with a smirk.

We drove down to US Auto Finance to see if we can find a decent used car for Braydon. We pulled up to the lot, walked around and Jacob noticed something right away.

"Beth, look." He said while pointing in the direction of a dark blue 2009 Honda Civic with chrome wheels and a spoiler on the back.

"Oh my god!" I exclaimed as I walked towards the car. "It's perfect!"

No sooner had I said that, a tall, slender man comes out of the sales office and asks if we need any help. We told him we wanted to test drive the Honda Civic and he went back in to get us the keys. He handed them to Jacob and I got in the passenger side. About 1 minute into the test drive, after we had drove a bit down the empty dirt road, Jacob stops the car and pulls over.

"Something wrong with the car?" I asked.

"No." he answered. Then he leans over and starts making out with me. We are making out! In my sons potentially new car. And I didn't stop him. Not until things started getting a little too hot and heavy. I pulled away and told him we needed to head back. We smiled at each other and then he drove back to the lot. We told the man there that we wanted the car and we started on the paperwork right away. Jacob actually got him to lower the price. He was good at that too apparently.

After everything was signed and done, I asked him to drive Braydon's car back to the house. We actually raced each other down the deserted road until we got into town. It was so much fun and reckless. Something I only experience with Jacob. It's exhilarating if I hadn't said that already. I texted momma to let her know we were almost home. She messaged back saying that they were still in the yard doing some work and that she would keep Bray occupied.

I pulled into the driveway and Jacob soon followed. He got out of the car right after I got out of mine and gave me a huge embrace lifting me off the ground. I yelped a little because it caught me off guard. Then he slowly lowered me down and just stared into my eyes.

"God, I want to kiss you right now." He said tenderly.

"You better not." I replied.

"What's going on?" Braydon said with a somewhat angry voice. I guess it must have looked strange seeing me in Jacobs arms like that.

"Braydon." I said as I quickly straightened out my dress. "Where's momma?"

"Is something going on with you two?" Bray asked very disturbed.

"What? No." I quickly responded, "we were just...."

"Braydon." momma said out of breath strutting quickly from behind the house. "I told you to wait."

"What's going on?" He asked troubled.

"We wanted to surprise you." Jacob said.

"With what?" he questioned still a little unsure.

"With this." I said and pointed to the car. I guess Braydon couldn't see the car parked behind mine but when he came around to the back end, he saw the Honda Civic parked there and his jaw dropped.

"Whose is that? Is that car for me?" he asked with his tone finally shifting to excitement.

I shook my head 'yes' and his excitement took over. He kept saying 'No way.' about 5 times before coming up and hugging me.

"I had Jacob help me." I told him to try to cover things up. "That's why he's here."

"Oh, that's why you asked me about cars last night." Braydon said. "Clever sneak."

They did their handshake and Jacob replied, "That's me man, clever sneak."

My heart was beating a little fast because I felt like that was a close call. Braydon got in the car and ran the steering wheel through his fingers. I gave him the keys and told him to take care of it. "I will." He said. "J.T., get in."

Jacob looked at me then climbed into the passenger seat.

"We'll be back." Bray said. But just before they drove off, he got out of the car and gave me the biggest hug I had ever received from him and said, "Thanks mom."

My heart sank. Here I am lying to this poor boy and hiding my relationship from my entire family. All I ever wanted was for my kids to be happy. But I want to be happy too. Just never thought it would be like this. When I went back into the house, I was feeling pretty culpable. And momma must have caught on to it cause she asked, "So....did I hear Braydon ask you if something was going on between you and J.T.?"

"Oh," I started, a little tongue tied, "he hugged me when we got back. Guess he was excited for Bray getting his first car, too."

Momma walked up to me slowly, looked me in the eyes and then said with an ambiguous tone, "Yea. That must be it."

She walked away and headed towards the back door that led to her cottage. Does momma know something? Did Peggy tell anyone? That was really strange. And this is going too far. I have to figure out a way to tell my family. But I should really talk it over with Jacob first. I wasn't sure how long him and Bray would be gone but tomorrow is his birthday. And I still haven't figured out what I was going to do. It had to be spectacular. But it also has to be the night I tell him that I can't keep us secret anymore. The guilt is eating my alive.

Chapter 10

The next morning, I woke up suddenly with an idea of what to do for Jacob. Today was his birthday and I was determined to do something special. I had made reservations at this restaurant in Indianapolis that was really, really nice. But the idea I had was to play him a song on my daddy's guitar somehow, somewhere. When I was younger, he taught me how to play one song and I think I still remember it. There was this one time in California when I went to a college party with Mitch and there was a guitar on a stand at the guy's house we were at. I started to play that song and Mitch told me to knock it off. I never played it since. But I'm sure it's like riding a bike and you never forget. I threw the covers off me and went to the cottage shed, since that's where momma said she put some of daddy's things. I started searching and digging through the large boxes and under clothes. But there was no guitar. I looked behind stuff, under stuff, but no guitar.

"What are you doing?" momma said frightening me.

"I was just looking for daddy's old guitar." I replied

"What on earth for?" she asked.

I thought for a second then said, "Just to see if I could remember how to play that one song he taught me."

"Oh sweetheart." She started with a disquiet look on her face.

"What?" I asked unsure.

"I donated it to the community closet a couple years ago with some of his other things." she told me.

"Seriously?" I said disappointed. There goes that idea.

"I'm sorry." she said softly.

I sat on one of the boxes thinking about what I was going to do now that was more special than reservations at a fancy restaurant.

"Why do you have all this stuff still anyways?" I asked.

"I don't know." she responded. "I guess cause it's all I have left of him to hold on to."

She paused for a moment, then continued, "I suppose I thought if I get rid of the rest of his things, then that meant I was finally getting rid of him."

I stood up, slowly walked over to her and said, "He'll always be with you momma. His stuff is not him." Then I gave her a hug and a smile.

"I guess I'll put everything back." I stated and started picking up the boxes.

"Actually, " she began. "I think it's time we donate the rest."

"You sure?" I questioned.

She looked around the room then responded, "Yea. Yea I'm sure."

We started to pile everything in the back of daddy's old truck which she still had, surprisingly. She started it up and I was amazed that it still ran. I told her I would go inside to let Braydon know we were heading to the thrift store and we would be back later. I went back outside, hopped in the passenger seat and we were off. As we headed down the driveway, I saw Jacob outside mowing the lawn at the Miller house. He waved and momma waved back while I just smiled. Then mom started telling me some things I had never known before. "You know, your daddy was 11 years younger than me when we met."

"Are you serious?" I asked.

"Mmhmm." she responded while shaking her head yes. "I rejected him over and over. I would say things to him like 'You're just a kid.' or asked him if he needed his diaper changed. I was so mean to him. Yet he never gave up. I kept thinking, 'I am a 30-year-old woman and he is a 19-year-old kid, teenager in fact. What on earth could he possibly have to offer me? But I'm glad I gave him a chance. And when you came along shortly after, he promised me that he would always do everything and anything he could to take care of us. And he did. He was an amazing man."

I just watched her as she told me this information that I never even knew. I never questioned how old daddy was cause him and momma were always so close. And growing up we never celebrated birthdays with candles. We always just did things together as a family on those days. No one ever talked about age. Which its weird that I am so concerned about it.

"Anyway, Jacob just made me think of that." she finished by saying.

I looked at her puzzled and asked, "Why?"

"Cause he reminds me a lot of him." she said.

I looked out the window and just got lost in my own thoughts. Is she trying to tell me something? Should I just tell her what's going on and how I feel? It seems to me like she'd understand. I really can't wait to talk to Jacob about this first so we can get all of this out in the open. We pull up to the Community Closet and Andrew Michael Blackman came walking out. He was just a little boy last time I saw him.

"Miss Mary Beth?" he stated.

"Well I'll be. Little Andy." I responded.

"I always hated when you called me that." he said with a smirk and came over to give me a hug.

"It's nice to see you." he added.

"You too. You're all grown up." I said.

"Be 17 this year." He mentioned with a proud tone.

"Practically an adult." I responded.

"Mind helping us with these boxes Andy?" Momma asked him.

"Sure thing Mrs. Harper. Got more things to donate, I see." he said while starting to unload.

I asked him if he knew about daddy's guitar and if it was still here. He asked his mom when we walked in the store who was working behind the counter and was just as enthusiastic to see me as he was. But she proceeded to tell me that someone picked up that guitar only several months ago.

"Oh. Oh well. I'm glad someone is getting use out of it." I said feeling bummed.

While we were there, my phone rang and it was Bella asking to come home. Apparently, the parents of the friend's house she was staying at had to go somewhere important soon, so she needed me to pick her up. Momma said we could swing by and get her since she was only a couple of blocks away. When we pulled up to this house, she come running out excited to see me.

"Do I get to ride in the back?" she asked with her eyes wide open.

"Hop in." I responded.

She jumped in the back and yelled "Woo Hoo!" and held on to the side of the truck bed. We headed home and every once in a while, I would look back to make sure she was ok. Her eyes were closed, and her other hand was waving around in the air. I smiled and thought about how happy my kids seem since we moved here. And I'm about to drop a bomb.

When we got home, Bella ran inside and straight to the couch to turn on the tv. I went and checked on Bray and he was doing what he always does in his room. So, I told everyone I was going to lay down for a bit since I was tired from all the work. I went in my room and shut the door. I pulled out a notebook and a pencil and sat on my bed. Maybe I can write Jacob a poem? But every sentence that I wrote was so dumb and cheesy that I would scribble it out and toss the piece of paper to the floor all crumpled up. I couldn't think of anything. All the romantic gestures he's done for me and all the wonderful things we had talked about and I could not think of one single line to write. I threw the paper and pencil on the floor and let out a sigh. Then my phone went off. I looked to see there was a text from Jacob that read, "My folks left to go out of town for a few days. Can you come over around 5?" At first, I felt bad that his parent's had left him there on his birthday. Then I remembered our reservations were at 6:30. So that was half an hour of alone time before we had to leave for Indianapolis and that was perfect. "I'll be there." I replied with a wink face. And he sent back a red heart.

I actually tried to take a little nap cause I was exhausted from loading all those boxes. I ended up snoozing for about an hour and was awakened by my phone ringing. It was Peggy Sue. She was asking me if I wanted to have dinner with them over at their place tonight. But obviously I told her I had other plans. And then, a thought came into my head that I should feel guilty about, but I didn't. And that was, I can use this as an excuse to leave the house. This is the last and final lie before I finally talk to Jacob about us coming out.

We hung up the phone and I went into the living room where momma was sitting on the chair reading the paper and Bella was on the couch watching tv.

"How was your nap?" Bella asked with her sweet voice.

"It was nice sweet pea." I replied. Then I went on to tell them both. "Uh, Peggy just called. Asked if I wanted to come over to their house for dinner tonight."

"Can I come?" Bella jumped up and asked. She loves kids and Peggy has a whole daycare.

"No, I'm sorry baby. It's just adults this time." I said." The kids are at grandmas, so she wants to have a fancy wine party."

"Oh, that sounds fun. You gonna go?" Momma said and asked.

"Yea. I was thinking about it." I responded. "Would that be alright?"

"Of course." Momma said. "Maybe I can teach Bella how to play bridge."

Bella got excited and I thanked her for watching the kids. I went back towards my room to get ready and popped in to Braydon's room for a sec.

"Hey." I said as I knocked on the door which was part way open.

"I heard." he said.

"Heard what?" I asked.

"You're going to Peggy's." He replied.

"Is that ok with you?" I asked him.

"I don't care. I'll just be here playing since J.T. is busy tonight too." He stated not even looking at me but instead focused on his game.

"Oh, sorry to hear that." I said. "Well, at least come out later and have dinner with momma and Bella."

"Ok." he responded.

I shut the door quietly and still felt like he knew something. But I wasn't sure how. I began to think about how I was going to tell Jacob that we needed to come clean. Should I tell him at dinner? On the drive to the restaurant? I was nervous and scared to confess everything to my family. I didn't want them to hate me. Especially Bray. He was always there for me when someone hurt me. He was there to help cook and clean and run errands with my car in the past. Anything I asked him to do, he would do it, usually without complaining. And this is the thanks he gets. I took a deep breath and went back to my room. I changed into a little black dress that buttoned all the way down the front. I put on some black strappy heels and then my lipstick. I headed out of my room when Bella caught sight of me and exclaimed, "Woah hot momma."

I laughed and thanked her while giving her a hug.

"Wow, you look fancy." momma said with a wondering look on her face.

"She said dress nice." I responded.

"Well, have a good time." momma said.

I left the house and got in my car because I couldn't possibly walk to Jacob's house. I drove down the street a little ways and parked behind some bushes. Then I proceeded to walk to his house with haste hoping no one would see me. When I reached the front door, I took a deep breath then knocked.

He yelled "Come in." from the inside so I opened the door and there he stood, in front of the dining table that was adorned with a red tablecloth, tons of candles and a place setting for 2. As I walked closer, I looked and saw there were candles everywhere. And Jacob looked so handsome. He was wearing a navy-blue suit, tan dress shoes, white button-down shirt and a tan colored tie. His hands were behind him and he had such a come-hither look on his face.

"What is all this?" I said with a smile and tears in my eyes.

As I got closer, he pulled his hands from behind him and one hand was holding a single sunflower. He handed it to me and said, "I wanted you to know just how much you mean to me."

I was taken back by this as I took the sunflower from his hand. After I thanked him, I said, "But it's your birthday. And you did all this for me? I didn't even get you a present. I just made reservations at Vida's."

"Well, cancel them." He said as he put his arms around my waist. "You're the only present I need."

He leaned in and gave me a slow, passionate kiss. Then he pulled out my chair and had me sit down. He went into the kitchen and came out with 2 plates that he set in front of me and in front of his chair. He opened the bottle of wine and poured it in each glass.

"Is this your first time having wine?" I asked with a sarcastic tone.

"As a matter of fact, yes." He replied and we both started to laugh.

"Mmm, this smells delicious." I stated as I admired my plate. "Did you make this?"

"I did." he replied. "Tonight, you will be feasting on rosemary and lemon garlic chicken with wild mushroom rice and steamed green beans."

"Fancy." I responded.

He lifted his glass and I lifted up mine.

"Here's to us." He began. "May there be many more birthdays that I get to spend with you." He clanked my glass and we said "Cheers."

After taking a sip of our wine, I took a bite of my chicken when he said to me, "So, I don't like wine."

We laughed and just enjoyed each other's company. I had mentioned that I couldn't believe his parents weren't here for his birthday. But apparently, he had told them he had plans out of town with friends so that's why they left. They had some important business to attend to in Washington and didn't feel bad leaving since he would be busy.

"This meal is absolutely delicious." I stated.

He smiled and looked me in my eyes, just staring for a while. He cooks, he's a hard worker, he's romantic and smart, funny and charming. I couldn't have asked for more. After we were done eating, we decided to go into the living room. When he sat down on the couch, I walked over to the guitar and picked it up.

"Whatcha doin?" he asked clueless.

I sat on the chair opposite of the couch and held the guitar like one does when they are about to play.

"My daddy taught me a song when I was 10." I began. "So, I wanted to try and play it for you."

"Are you serious?" he asked with even more lust in his eyes.

I nodded my head 'yes' and finished by saying, "It's been years. So, bear with me."

He smiled in anticipation. Then his jaw hit the floor as I started playing. But when I started singing, his face lit up and I swear he even got choked up a few times. The song I learned to play was "When

You Say Nothing at All" by Alison Krause. When I finished playing, he just sat there staring at me.

"Sorry, that was terrible." I began, but he instantly cut me off.

"No, it wasn't. It was amazing." He said soft spoken and in awe.

I smiled a bashful smile and looked down at the floor. When I pushed my hair back from my face, I noticed something on the back of the guitar that looked oddly familiar. *"To my love and my life, you're the melody to my song."* This was my daddy's guitar. It had to be. How many people could possibly inscribe those same words on a guitar?

"Where did you get this guitar?" I asked with extreme curiosity.

"At a thrift store in town." he replied. "When I first moved here mine got broke in the move and..."

"This is my daddy's guitar." I said interrupting.

"What?" he asked while walking over to me.

"Yea, see?" I said as I showed him the inscription. "My momma had that done for him."

"Oh my god." He responded in shock. "What are the chances?"

He paused for a moment while I was still looking over the guitar thoroughly and continued saying, "That show's me that we were meant to be."

I looked up at him and smiled. I nodded my head and thought 'He's so silly.' Then he asked me, "You want to go swimming?"

"What?" I asked while laughing. But when I looked at him, he wasn't joking, "oh, you're serious?"

He held out his hand and I stated, "But I don't have a suit."

"Who needs a suit?" he responded and winked.

I slowly took his hand and he led me to the pool in the back yard. It was completely fenced in and hidden by trees so I knew no one will see us. He started to take off his shirt and tie, then his pants and finally his socks. He looked at me and smiled then jumped right in. When he came up out of the water, he asked me, "You coming?"

I rolled my eyes and replied, "You're insane." as I slowly took off my shoes, then unbuttoned the front of my dress. Once I removed it, I dove in and immediately regretted it.

"Oh my god, it's cold." I said shivering as I came up out of the water. "It's so cold."

"Here, I'll warm you up." he said as he swam over to me and wrapped his arms around me.

"That better?" he asked softly while looking in my eyes.

"Getting there." I responded. Then I started to lean in to kiss him and just before I did, I said, "But this might be warmer."

We started to kiss then he lifted me up out of the water and I wrapped my legs around his waist. The kissing started to get more and more intense. We could quietly hear the music in the living room that he had playing during dinner. But before anything further could happen, I heard someone's voice that scared the crap out of me.

"What the .....?" the voice said.

I suddenly turned around and to my very upset surprise, it was Braydon.

"Oh my god." I said quickly hurrying to swim back to the edge of the pool.

"Unbelievable." Braydon said angrily and started running back toward the house.

"Braydon WAIT!" I exclaimed. I started to fumble for my clothes and button up my dress while yelling his name repeatedly. Jacob was also getting out and grabbed a towel. Soaking wet, I started running after Bray still calling his name.

"Elizabeth!" Jacob screamed. But I didn't stop. I kept chasing after Bray desperate to catch up.

"Braydon please." I yelled again starting to cry.

"Leave me alone!" he screamed back. And he wouldn't turn around. He ran into our house and I was almost to the driveway. When I finally got inside, he had already grabbed his keys and was heading back out.

"Braydon please. Can we talk about this?" I said with tears starting to stream down my face as I tried to grab his arm.

"Get away from me!." he said with aggression and pushed me to the ground.

"Braydon!" momma yelled in the background upset at what she just saw.

He ran out the door and got in his car locking it quickly behind him. I followed him out still crying and still calling out his name. But he zoomed out of the driveway and at that time there was Jacob with my purse, my shoes and with his shirt unbuttoned walking up the lawn.

"What's going on?" momma asked as she came out of the house.

I snatched my purse from Jacobs hands and ran to my car which was parked down the street. I heard momma and Jacob both yell my name, but my focus was on finding Bray. As fast as I possibly could, I ran to my car and got in. But Jacob was right behind me.

"Elizabeth! Stop!" Jacob yelled as I tried to drive away. But the windows were rolled down, and he put his hands on the car door stopping me.

"Jacob, please." I said while still crying. I kept braking and going but he wouldn't let go of the car. He kept begging me to let him come.

"Jacob. Go home!!!" I screamed. Then I looked at him and said with a low and somber tone. "Go home. You've done enough."

Jacob looked at me, baffled as to why I was putting the blame on him. He slowly let go of the car and I drove away. I didn't even look back, but I knew he was just standing there, wondering exactly what he did wrong. But that didn't matter right now. Braydon was all that mattered at the moment. I have to find him. He can't drive in this state of mind. As I headed down the road in the direction he went, I was crying uncontrollably, thinking the whole time that I shouldn't have let this happen. I should have ended things with Jacob from the very beginning. I sped down main street and off in the distance I saw Braydon's car getting on the interstate. Oh god no, please don't, I thought.

I raced to the exit and started weaving in and out of traffic just as Braydon was doing about a half a mile in front of me. I started beeping my horn, but he would only drive faster. My phone kept ringing, too. First momma, then Jacob and he called multiple times. But I wouldn't answer. I finally put my phone on silent and threw it in the back seat almost losing control of the car. Then, just as I was regaining control of my car, Braydon lost control of his. It was like everything was happening in slow motion as I watched him skid across 3 lanes of traffic, hitting the guard rail and flying over the edge of the overpass. I let out the most gut-wrenching scream and witnessed his car flip 4 times and land in the brush below. I was crying hysterically and all I could do was pull over, get out of my car that I left in the middle of the highway and run to him. Just before I was about to climb over the rail, a by passer who saw the whole thing tried to stop me. But I pushed him off me and continued sliding down the hill, screaming Braydon's name over and over.

When I got to his car, it was mangled, almost torn in 2, smoking from the hood which was completely pushed in. The air bag was deployed, and Bray was unconscious. He had blood coming from his forehead and his ear and his legs were trapped under the steering wheel. I could hear people in the distance coming towards me.

"Somebody help!" I shrieked. "Please. Call an ambulance."

I just held his hand and while trying to calm myself down, I said, "It's gonna be ok. Everything is going to be ok." But he didn't answer. He just laid there motionless. Tears continued to stream down my cheeks. This is undeniably all my fault and the worst pain I have ever felt. Please don't let him die, I said to myself. I could hear the sirens muffled in the background as they got closer and closer. One of the emergency crew pulled me away and I watched as they tore his door off with the jaws of life. They started asking me questions, but again, it was like my body was there and my mind wasn't.

"That's my son, Braydon." was all I could say.

They carefully placed a brace around his neck and lifted him on to the stretcher. I grabbed his hand again and walked beside him as they put him in to the back of the ambulance. Then I prayed. That's all I could do. Please God, let him be ok. Please.

Chapter 11

Beep.......beep......beep......beep.

That's the sound I heard from the heart monitor as I sat next to Braydon who was lying in a hospital bed, covered with a blanket and tubes coming from everywhere. I haven't stopped crying. I haven't slept. I've just been praying and hoping he'll be ok. This is the worst thing a parent could ever go through. I just sat there holding his hand, rubbing it in hopes he would wake up. I kept wishing I could be the one laying there instead, wanting to take his place. Just then, I heard someone coming in through his room door. It was momma, holding a bag and balloons that said "Get well."

"Momma." I said after running to her and hugging her, immediately crying harder than before.

"I'm here baby." momma responded while rubbing my back.

"Any news yet?" She asked.

I just shook my head 'no'. Momma went and put the balloons by the bed. She ran her fingers through his hair then gently kissed his forehead.

"I brought you a change of clothes, your phone charger and some things." momma said as she handed me the bag,

"Thanks." I told her. She sat down in the chair on the other side of Braydon and just looked at him with worry. I put the bag down and sat down in the chair that I was sitting in before on his other side.

"Where's Bella?" I asked momma.

"I dropped her off at the Jenkin's place." she responded. "I just told her Braydon wasn't feeling good and had to get some tests done."

I was happy she told her that. I didn't want her to know about the accident and that Bray was really hurt. It would totally break her. Silence filled the room and dismay came over me.

"Wanna talk?" momma asked calmly.

I shook my head 'no' while beginning to cry again but trying so hard to hold back the tears.

"It may help." momma added.

"What's there to say momma?" I began. "I didn't mean for this to happen. I just wanted to be loved by someone."

Momma stood up and pulled her chair over next to me. She put her arm around my shoulder and said, "I love you. Braydon loves you. Bella loves you. Isn't that enough?"

"Of course it is momma. But look at Braydon. This is all my fault."

"Did you lie? Yes. Did you keep secrets from your family? Absolutely." momma said

"This is not making me feel better." I said cutting her off.

"But," she interrupted, "Braydon chose to get in his car and drive reckless."

"Cause of me." I added.

"Maybe so, but accidents happen." She continued. "Don't beat yourself up. You're only human."

The nurse came in and was checking Braydon's vitals. She was adjusting his pillow and checking the tubes. The doctor soon followed and me and momma both stood up eager to hear what he had to say.

"Well," the doctor started. "He's gonna be ok."

Momma and I both took a big sigh of relief, smiled and hugged each other.

"The bleeding in his brain has subsided so I'm going to wake him up from his induced coma." The doctor told us. "He should be awake in about an hour. If you don't mind stepping into the waiting room, we'll come get you shortly."

Momma and I stepped outside the door and when I looked up, the entire waiting room was filled with half the town. There was Peggy and Billy, Laura Lynn and Little Andy. I couldn't believe all the people who came out to support us. Once again, I started to cry. Momma leaned into me and said gently, "Do you see how many people love you?" I smiled and tried to hold back the tears. Everyone there was waiting with anticipation to see how Braydon was doing.

"He's gonna be ok." I told them.

Everyone cheered and started hugging one another. Then they came to me and each person started hugging me one by one. A part of me felt so relieved. I mean, of course I'm so happy Braydon is going to be alright. But the other part of me was still riddled with guilt. I sat down in one of the chairs and momma sat on my left side. I started rubbing my forehead because of the headache I developed from all the crying and lack of sleep. Peggy came and sat down on my other side while momma started rubbing my neck. But I couldn't stay seated for long. Waiting was making me crazy. So I got up and paced the room for about 10 minutes then went to the vending machine to get a coffee. But out of the corner of my eye, I saw someone walking toward me. It was Jacob.

"Elizabeth." he said as he got closer.

I turned around and dropped my coffee which startled me and I jumped. Jacob ran up and offered to help. But I stopped him and said, "You can't be here Jacob."

"Why not?" he asked. "I want to be here for you and him. He's my friend."

"But he's my son!" I exclaimed. "You being here will only make things worse."

"But Beth..." he began.

"Please go." I begged him. But he paused for a moment and replied, "No. I'm not leaving, either of you."

Just then the doctor came out and said he was awake. He told me that only me and momma could go in at that moment. I turned around and looked at Jacob and gave him this look hoping he would take the hint and leave. But he didn't. He walked over to the waiting room and sat down.

When I walked into the room, Braydon was still laying there and all the tubes were gone. He saw me and he instantly looked away in disgust.

"I'll leave you two alone." momma said as she rubbed my back then walked out the door.

I slowly walked over to Braydon and sat down on the bed next to him. I tried to grab his hand, but he just pulled it away quickly. I could feel the tears welling up in my eyes, but I had to fight it. If I let them out, I knew I wouldn't be able to speak.

"How are you feeling?" I asked.

"How do you think I'm feeling?" he replied with irritation and exhaustion in his voice. "I was in a car wreck."

I took a long pause for a moment then I started to speak.

"Braydon." I began. "I know there's nothing I can say...."

But he cut me off abruptly and said, "No there isn't. Sorry won't even cut it."

I looked at my feet and silence spoke for a bit. Then he continued.

"You lied to me. You lied to everyone. And then I walked in on my best friend making out with my....." he stopped cause he couldn't even finish the sentence. I could tell he was angry and disappointed at the same time. But he was also in a lot of pain, both physically and mentally. Then his eyes also began to fill with tears. So, he turned his head the other direction and just stared out the window. I saw a tear roll down his cheek and the flood gates opened for me.

"I know saying I'm sorry isn't good enough." I began. "But I'm going to say it anyway."

At that point I was sobbing but I had to get this out.

"I'm so, so sorry that I lied to you. I'm so sorry that I hurt you. But I am willing to do whatever it may take to get you to trust me again. I should have never let this happen. But from the bottom of my heart Braydon, I truly and deeply regret any pain that I have caused you."

He sat there breathing heavy still staring out the window. But then he finally slowly turned his head and looked at me. Then he said between shallow breathes...

"I never want you to see him again." He began. I agreed and he continued. "I don't ever want to see him again. So, I want to move."

"But we just got here." I said.

"I don't care." He responded. "You said you'd do anything. So, I wanna move."

I shook my head 'yes' in agreement, but my heart sank. Bella was finally happy to be close to momma. I was happy to be close to momma. Braydon was happy until I screwed up. But if this is what it takes to earn his trust again, then it has to be done. I could also tell he was getting very agitated because his heart rate on the monitor was starting to get faster.

"He really needs to take it easy." Said the nurse as she walked over to him.

"I'm fine." He replied to the nurse. She walked away and he continued.

"You're gonna fix my car." He said.

"I was planning on doing that anyway." I told him.

"Good." He replied.

"Is there anything else?" I asked.

"Yes." He began. "Don't lie to me, ever again."

"I won't." I responded softly.

He looked out the window again and then back at me. I was just staring at the floor when he reached over and grabbed my hand. I looked up at him with tears in my eyes then he said, "I love you mom."

"I love you, too." I cried as I got up and hugged him. And sure enough, he gave me one of his Braydon half-assed side hugs. But that's ok. It's a step in the right direction.

"We're gonna get through this." I said.

Momma must have been listening by the door because she peeked her head in and said, "Can I come in now?"

We smiled and Braydon told her to come on. She hugged him and they started talking about the accident and how he was feeling. I gave a little smile and for a second felt like everything was going to be ok. Then I remembered Jacob was in the other room.

"I'll be right back." I said as I headed toward the door. I went into the waiting room and I told everyone he was awake and that they could see him a few at a time. I looked at Jacob and said, "Not you though." Everyone kind of turned their heads acting like they weren't listening.

"What? Beth?" he started but I wouldn't let him finish.

"Jacob. Please." I pleaded. "It's Braydon's wishes"

I began walking away and didn't turn around. I just headed into Braydon's room and allowed Peggy and Billy to follow me in. Peggy rubbed my back and smiled. But I couldn't smile. The pain of sending Jacob away and the pain of seeing Braydon hurt in a hospital bed as well as just agreeing never to see Jacob again plus agreeing to move, was all so overwhelming. The next few hours were kind of in fast forward as so many people came in and out to check on Braydon. I decided to sleep in the hospital with him for the next few days cause I didn't want to leave his side. Those few days were so exhausting. I didn't get much sleep. For one, the couch there was super uncomfortable and two, my mind wouldn't shut up.

"Mom?" Braydon said on the 4th night at about 9:30 pm. "Why don't you go home?"

"No champ, I won't leave you." I replied as I walked over to him and took his hand.

"It's ok mom. I shouldn't be here much longer. You need some sleep. I'll be fine." He said.

I gave him a smile and kissed his forehead.

"I'll come by every day." I told him which made him smile.

I started to gather up my clothes and other things that were there. And as I was packing the bag, Braydon asked me, "Mom? Promise me something."

"Sure baby. Anything." I responded.

"Promise me you won't see J.T. when you go back home?"

I looked at him and promised that I wouldn't. But deep down inside I really wanted to. Just to set some things right. But a promise is a promise. I have to keep my word. Although, I know Jacob is going to be watching the house like a hawk to see when I get home. And sure enough, the second I got back to the house there was a knock at the door. Momma answered and I could barely hear Jacob on the other side. But momma told him, "Jacob. You have to respect me. Please. This is my house." Then a few seconds later she shut the door and came into the living room to sit next to me on the couch.

"You ok?" she asked. I just shook my head 'yes'.

Momma didn't say another word and left the room. What can she say? This was all such a mess. The next day I went into the cottage shed to gather any empty boxes I could find so I could start packing. I found quite a few and began in my bedroom. As I was packing some things, there was a knock at the door. I hope that's not Jacob again, I thought. But when momma answered, I heard that sweet southern voice getting louder and louder as it got closer to my room.

"Feels like we were just here unpacking." Peggy said as she entered my room.

I walked over to her and gave her a big hug, trying not to start crying.

"What are you doing here?" I asked.

"Well, your momma texted me. Said you was moving again." She replied. "I must admit I don't like the idea. But I understand why. So, I wanna help."

I smiled then we proceeded to grab some boxes and headed to the kitchen. Momma came and decided to help as well. She brought some newspaper and set it on the table while I started taking glasses out of the cabinet. Then I sat down across from Peggy at the kitchen table and we started wrapping glasses.

"You know, Jacob's probably been by at least 20 times asking about both you and Braydon." Momma stated as she proceeded to take things out of the cabinets.

I looked at her with a 'why are you saying this' kind of look because Jacob needed to be the furthest thing from my mind right now.

"It's true." Peggy added. "Me and Billy Joe sat with momma while you were at the hospital one night and that hunk a man came by several times. He looked panicked for sure."

I looked at Peggy with the same look I gave momma then she continued,

"I told momma Harper I knew."

"Knew what? I never told you anything." I said to her.

"Honey, I ain't as dumb as I sound. I knew without you breathing a word."

I just sat there and stared at the floor while I listened to these two talk amongst themselves.

"He seems really sweet." Momma said. "And he seems to really adore you."

"He does." Added Peggy. "You could see it in his face when he said your name. Plus, he's so dreamy." She added with bashfulness in her voice as she sunk into her chair.

"Enough guys!" I exclaimed as I stood up from my seat. "It is not about Jacob and me right now. It's about Braydon and him getting better. Me and Jacob can never be. I made a promise to Bray."

I paused for a moment and it was so quiet you could hear a feather hit the floor. Then I continued to speak while trying to hold back tears, "Besides, I can't have kids anymore. He probably wants his own family. I can't give him that. And that doesn't even matter. All that matters right now is Braydon's happiness."

Momma stood up, looked me in the eyes after she walked over to me and said, "What about what makes YOU happy?" She looked at me for a few seconds with all seriousness then she walked away into another room. Peggy just looked at me and gave me a backwards smile. I crossed my arms and felt so flustered. How could they even talk about this? Braydon may be ok physically, but how is he going to be emotionally? Or mentally?

I walked into my room and sat on the bed. I started to cry while a million thoughts raced in my head. Of course, I want to be happy. And I feel in the depths of my soul that Jacob could definitely make me happy. I was the happiest I have ever been when I was with him. But Braydon comes first. His happiness is more important than mine. Isn't it?

"Knock knock." Peggy said as she peeked her head around the corner.

"I'm sorry." I replied while crying.

"Hey," she began as she walked over and sat next to me on my bed. "You have nothing to be sorry for. You've been through a lot."

She put her arms around me, and I put my head on her shoulder. Then momma came in the room and sat on the other side of me. She too put her arm around me and the 3 of us just sat there. "We love you, Beth." momma said. "And we just want what's best for you."

"For all of you." Peggy added.

"I know guys." I responded as I wiped the tears from my face. "I just don't know what that is right now."

"And that's ok if you don't know." Momma said. "But whatever you choose to do, we are here for you 100%. If you decide to move, we'll help you pack. If you decide to stay, then stay."

"Yea, Mary Beth," Peggy disclosed, "We'll stand by you no matter what."

It was nice to know they had my back. But that still didn't make the choices I had to make any easier. However, I do know that I gave Braydon my word. So, the decision to move still stands. I need to finish packing and make all the arrangements. I'm not quite sure where we are going yet, but we will figure it out. I will figure it out.

Chapter 12

One week had passed since I left Braydon at the hospital. And he's finally coming home today. Almost everything is packed and ready to go. I made a reservation for movers to come the day after we leave so Jacob doesn't see the van and try to stop us. Speaking of Jacob, he hasn't tried to come by since momma asked him to respect her wishes. He texted me a couple times but it's been a few days since he has. It's also been very hard for me not to go and see him. I miss him so much. They say absence makes the heart grow fonder and for me, it really has. I've cried myself to sleep almost every night this week. But I'm sure once we move to North Carolina, it will get better and easier. That's where I decided to go. I remember I went there once with Mitch for a college thing and I fell in love with the state. I loved the mountains and the trees, the weather was perfect in the middle of the summer. But I've never been back since.

When I arrived at the hospital, Braydon was all dressed and ready to go, sitting in a wheelchair by the receptionist's desk.

"Hey there champ." I said to him as I walked towards him.

This time when he saw me, his face lit up.

"Mom." He said with a smile.

I leaned over and kissed his cheek then signed some papers for his release.

"Ready to go?" I asked.

"Absolutely." He responded.

I wheeled the chair down the hall and out the front door of the hospital. A male nurse was outside waiting to help me with getting Braydon in the car. They gave me his crutches that he had to be on for a few weeks and I put them in the back seat. I thanked the man and we were on our way.

The ride home was pretty quiet. I wasn't sure what he was thinking. We talked a lot in the hospital about life and things he went through emotionally between Mitch and Jefferey. I never knew how he felt before. He never told me. He always kept things in, but he made promises too. One promise was to be more open with me. So, I tried to get him to do just that.

"So." I began. "Anything you want to talk about?"

He sat there for a minute and I could tell he was thinking. Then he responded.

"Did you decide where we're going to move?"

"I did." I said. "I chose North Carolina. Everything's all set. We leave Friday."

"This Friday?" he asked.

"Yes, why?"

"My birthday is next Saturday." he replied.

"Oh." I said sadly knowing momma was not going to be a part of it.

"It's ok. I'm ready to get out of here." Braydon said.

I gave him a melancholy smile and just focused on the road. When we pulled up to the driveway, momma and Bella were there with a sign Bella had made that said, "Welcome Home Brat." When Braydon caught sight of it, he laughed and said, "She's such a turd."

He got out of the car and I helped him with his crutches. He started to hobble towards the door when Bella ran over to him and hugged him tight. And he actually hugged her back.

"Welcome home young man." Momma said as she hugged him too.

I grabbed his bag out of the car that I had packed and brought to him when he was in the hospital. I took it in the house and he immediately walked in his room. I shook my head and thought, 'That didn't take long.' I guess he missed his video games more than us.

"How was the ride home?" momma asked as I sat on the kitchen chair.

"It was mostly quiet." I replied. "I told him where we were moving and when."

"What did he say?"

"He seemed a little bummed that we were leaving before his 18th birthday."

"Aww poor kid." Momma responded. "Hey, maybe we should bake him a cake and have it before you go."

"That's a good idea momma. He'd love that."

She smiled and proceeded to finish making her tea. I went over to his room and knocked on the door asking if I could come in. He was just lying in his bed as he said 'yes'.

"You need anything?" I asked.

"No, I'm ok." he replied.

"Well, if you need me just holler." I said as I started to close his door.

"Hey mom?" Braydon said before I walked out.

"Yes champ?" I responded as I turned to look at him.

"Tell grandma to make it chocolate."

He smiled and I smiled back because apparently, he heard us talking about the cake. So, I made sure to let momma know his request.

The next morning, I had made some breakfast for Braydon and brought it in to his room. I also made some snacks and a sandwich for him during the day to keep in the fridge while I'm at the shop working on his cake.

"You sure you don't want me to stay home?" I asked him as I set his breakfast on the table next to his bed.

"I'll be fine mom. I'll call you if I need you." He replied.

I told him about his lunch and snacks in the fridge and then was on my way. Bella went with me to the shop since it was spring break and there was no school. When I got to the shop, momma was already there taking Braydon's cake out of the oven. I loved the smell of this place. I'm sure going to miss working here.

Later in the day, while I was decorating his cake and Bella was at the table coloring, I had this feeling come over me like someone was watching me. When I slowly looked up, I could see Jacob standing by the tree outside looking in through the window. He waved and looked so sad. I waved back and he started walking towards the shop. But I shook my head 'no' and he stopped. He just stood there staring at me. It looked like he was about to cry but then he slowly backed away and just left.

My heart was racing in my chest. I closed my eyes and it took everything I had to not stop what I was doing and run to him. I wanted so badly to say goodbye, but I couldn't. No more sneaking around. No more lies. I've already disappointed Braydon so much. I just have to move on.

That rainy night, after we had dinner and cleaned up the kitchen, Braydon and Bella were sitting in the living room with Peggy, Billy and her kids. I had asked them to come by before we left. Momma lit the candles on Braydon's cake and turned off all the lights. I carried it into the living room and we all started singing Happy Birthday.

When Braydon blew out the candles, everyone clapped, and momma turned the lights back on. I sliced the cake and served everyone there. It was a nice little early celebration before I moved out of this town again.

"So, have you found a place to live yet?" Asked Peggy.

"Yes." I answered. "It's a cute little place just outside of Raleigh. And there's several bakeries in the area I could apply."

"That sounds good." Peggy responded.

Just then, Braydon's face turned cold as he looked up and said with a very indignant tone, "What the hell are you doing here?"

I turned around and there was Jacob, standing by the doorway, soaking wet from the rain.

"Jacob." I said as I stood up to look at him.

"There are things that I need to say." Jacob started. "And you're both going to listen."

"Get the hell out of my house." Braydon said trying to stand up, still furious that Jacob was there. I tried to stop him from standing but he wouldn't listen.

"Braydon!" Jacob said loudly, "This is not just your house. And I'm sorry Mrs. Harper for disrespecting your wishes." He said as he looked at momma. Then he turned back towards me and Bray and continued, "But I had to see both of you. You need to know Bray, that I am head over heels, completely and deeply in love with your mother. But I love you too man. We've become the best of friends. But so has your mom and I. And I can't lose you. But I can't lose her either."

I just stared at Jacob with tears filling up my eyes shaking my head in confusion. He walked closer to me and stood right in front of me.

"I can't live without you Beth." Jacob said in a gentle soft tone. "These past few weeks I've been lost without you. I want to spend my life with you, and I want to be in all of your lives forever. So, there's something I need to ask you."

Peggy Sue gasped and covered her mouth with her hands. Jacob started to get down on one knee but before he could even say, "Will you..." Braydon's fist came swinging around and he punched Jacob right in the nose. Jacob fell to the ground, Bella screamed, and I yelled Braydon's name.

"I told you to get the hell out." Braydon said raising his voice as I kept holding him back from trying to hit Jacob again. Even Billy Joe was holding on to Bray cause he had stumbled over this way without his crutches. Braydon kept yelling for him to get out, I was crying and begging him to stop, momma went over to Jacob to check on him and I just lost it. So, I screamed at the top of my lungs, "I LOVE HIM!"

Everyone froze in their tracks. Braydon stared at me baffled at what had I just said. So, I made sure to repeat it for everyone to hear.

"I love him, Bray." I said while crying.

"You do? You love me?" Jacob asked.

I turned around and looked at him still on the floor with a bloody nose.

"Yes Jacob." I said. "I love you."

Jacob's face lit up like the sun and made the whole room shine with his gorgeous smile. He rose to his feet and leaned in to kiss me but I stopped him by putting my hand over his mouth and said, "but you and I can never be."

He looked in my eyes and I could see my reflection in his because they were filled with tears.

"Elizabeth. Don't." he said in a whisper.

"I'm sorry." I responded under my breath. "But you have to go."

He looked around at everyone in the room, then back at me, and finally he quietly turned around and left. I stood there breathing heavy and crying. I turned around and looked at Braydon who still seemed so heated. Then I left the room, went to my bedroom and slammed the door. I didn't even care that I left everyone out in the living room without saying a word. Momma knocked on my door, but I told her to go away and I wanted everyone else to leave. I assumed Peggy and Billy left cause I heard the door shut and a car drive off.

I felt bad that I left momma to attend to the mess and to put Bella to bed as well as take care of Bray. But I just wanted to be alone. I sat in my chair curled up in a ball just staring out the window thinking about the events that just took place. He was going to propose to me. What an idiot. I told him I loved him. Because I do. I really do. It took me a while to realize it, but I couldn't hold it in any longer. This is not how things were supposed to turn out.

I heard Braydon slam his door and momma soon followed to talk to him. He yelled at her a couple of times and she raised her voice a bit. But then her tone became muffled. I'm not sure what she said to him, but it was quiet for a while.

That night I had a very hard time sleeping and I felt like a zombie the next day. I honestly don't remember most of that day. I do remember crawling in to bed early the next night and sleeping until the morning though. My body and mind are just exhausted. But that morning was the day we were heading to North Carolina. You could just feel the tension in the air. Everyone was quiet with discontent on their faces. And no one ate breakfast. So, we packed up the car as much as we could and started to say our goodbyes to momma.

"You're 1,000% sure this is what you want to do?" momma asked with tears in her eyes.

"I'm not sure of anything momma. But this has to be done. " I replied.

Bella ran to her one last time and gave her the biggest, tightest hug her little arms could give.

"Will you come visit us grandma?" Bella asked with sadness in her sweet little voice.

"Of course I will honey. As often as I can." momma responded.

We got in the car and I waved goodbye one more time then started backing out the driveway. As

I headed down Jefferson Street for the last time, I looked in my rear-view mirror to say goodbye again in my head. But when I looked, I saw Jacob standing at the end of his driveway watching us go. I silently began crying again but quickly wiped away my tears so Braydon wouldn't see.

The drive to North Carolina was painfully quiet. Both Bella and Bray either slept or had headphones in listening to something on their phones the entire ride. I had all the time in the world to think about everything that happened in the past 6 months and in my whole life. I wondered if I'd ever meet someone like Jacob again, if I would even be up to dating to find out. I turned on the radio to get these thoughts out of my head, but of course, every song reminded me of him. Every station I changed it to had a song that made me think of us. So, I turned it off with a bit of force and dissatisfaction.

"You ok?" Bray asked as he noticed me hit the radio.

"I'm fine. Just can't find a station I like." I replied.

We got to Raleigh North Carolina and stayed in a hotel for the night. The moving van wouldn't pick up our things till tomorrow so we had nothing in the new apartment just yet. Part of me was a little excited to actually see the new place. I rented it online and the pictures looked promising. But we will have to wait and see.

As Braydon took a shower and Bella laid on the hotel bed watching tv, I was on my laptop mapping out the things I had to do while we waited for the moving van. I had to register Bella at the new school, I had to explain to the high school why Braydon will be starting a new school just to graduate in a couple weeks, and I had to stop at a few bakeries to try and apply. I also had to look for a way to get Bray's car here once it was fixed. There was lots to do and I haven't even gotten settled in yet. So, I decided to try and get some sleep. Tomorrow I'm going to drive around and get a feel for our new town. I'll find the schools and the bakeries so come Monday morning, it'll be easier to get to where I needed to go. It's going to be a busy couple of days.

Chapter 13

"Hello?" I said as I answered the phone that Saturday morning.

It was the movers. And they called to tell me they were almost to our new apartment. Me and the kids had just got done driving around to find their schools and then had lunch. I told them they didn't have to actually start school until we got all settled in. We had already checked out of the hotel, so our bags were already with us in the car. We talked about a few of the bakeries I had went to but none of them were hiring and one was closed down.

"I'm sure you'll find something." Braydon assured me.

We finally arrived at the new apartment and the movers weren't there yet. So, I decided to go in and check it out in person. The landlord told me the key was in the lock box and gave me the code. It was a small complex with only 4 buildings but it was kept up really nice with tons of trees and flowers all around. When I got the key, I unlocked the door and saw it for the first time. Everything was white. White tile floors, white painted walls, white cabinets, and white appliances. It was old but still in good shape. It was 3 bedrooms and 2 baths. So, the kids went to put their bags in what would be their rooms. Finally, the movers arrived and started bringing everything in. Thank goodness the building was only one story because I was not in the mood for stairs.

I haven't slept great the past few weeks. How could I? All I could think about was the past 6 months with Jacob. I missed him so much. But I have to let go. After the movers got everything moved in, we looked at all of our stuff that was scattered throughout the apartment.

"Well, let's start with one box at a time." I said to the kids.

We each got started opening boxes and taking things out. It was a long couple of hours and an overall long day. At around 5:45 I suggested we stop and order some food. We ended up finding a Chinese place down the road who delivered. As we ate around the table surrounded by tons of empty and half unpacked boxes, silence filled the air. We were all kind of sad, even Bray. It was his desire to move again but he still seemed down.

"So." I started trying to break the ice. "What are everyone's thoughts?" But no one said anything.

"Come on guys. There has to be something you like about this place."

But still nothing. They just pushed their food around and stared at their plates.

"Ok, I'll start. I really like all the windows and the open floor plan."

But Braydon interrupted me saying, "Mom, just stop."

"Stop what?" I asked.

"Stop trying to pretend like everything is ok." He replied.

I took a deep breath and tried not to cry. I wasn't sure what else to say. Then Braydon got up and said, "I'm not hungry anymore." and walked to his new room shutting the door behind him. I looked at Bella and she looked like she was going to cry.

"Is Braydon ok?" she asked concerned.

"I don't know sweet pea." I replied. "I hope he is though."

"I miss grandma already." Bella said with a sad voice.

"Me, too." I responded.

"I miss Jacob." Bella added.

"Me, too." I responded softly. And then I lost my appetite. So, I got up, took my plate of food and threw it in the garbage. I started to cry while I leaned on the counter looking out the little window above the sink.

"Maybe you can call him." Bella said so sweetly.

"No baby girl." I responded while sniffling. "It's not that simple."

"Why isn't it?" she asked as she came over to me and wrapped her little arms around my waist.

"Oh, don't you worry your pretty little head about dumb adult stuff like that." I told her as I hugged her.

We just stood there, holding each other while I cried. I hope that we can get in a groove here and have a good life. I know it will take time. But patience was not on my side these days. The next few days was just us finishing unpacking and finding a spot for all our things. I started to hang some pictures on the wall when I got a text message. It was Jacob. He asked if I got there safe. I debated whether to text him back but I deleted everything I just typed out and turned off my phone. If I'm going to move on, I need to cut all ties. So, I deleted his name from my contacts and went back to what I was doing.

That Friday, after I dropped Bella off at the new school, I noticed an older gentleman hanging a sign on the front door of the bakery that was closed down. As I took a closer look, it said "Public Notice of Auction" on the sign. So I quickly parked the car to get out and talk to him.

"Excuse me." I yelled to the man. "What does that sign mean?"

He proceeded to tell me that the little old lady who owned the bakery died suddenly. The legality of it is she had no kin. Her husband passed away years prior and there was nothing in the will about the bakery. So, the city was going to sell it to the highest bidder at the auction that weekend. I started to wonder if it was possible for me to buy this place and have my own shop. I thanked the man then ran back to my car and went to my bank app on my phone. I noticed that I still had almost $20,000 in savings. I think tonight I will tell the kids my idea of buying it and see what they say. And to my surprise, they were all about it. While we were having dinner and actually eating this time, we discussed the details of the bakery.

"And you could work for me." I told Braydon.

"Well, that would be interesting." He responded and we both laughed.

The next night we found ourselves at the public auction building. We walked in and saw at least 40 people holding up numbered signs as the auctioneer spit off numbers faster than a hamster spinning on a wheel. I walked over to the registration booth and got my numbered sign. Me and the kids sat in the back row and waited about 35 minutes before it was time for the bakery to be auctioned off. He described the building and said everything in it was also included. So, he started the bidding at $5,000. A few minutes later a very masculine looking woman held up her sign and the auctioneer raised it to $6,000.

"Hold up your sign mom." Braydon said.

So, I did. The auctioneer raised it to $7,000 and the man lady raised her sign again. We went back and forth like that until it got up to $12,500 and she had the final say up to that point. I quickly logged in to my bank account again and saw that I had exactly $19,955. I did need some money to get things started and live on for at least a few months. But without hesitation, I stood up, raised my sign and said, "$16,000." The man lady looked back at me with a disgruntled look. But then she saw my kids and smiled. The auctioneer said, "$16,000 going once. Going twice. Sold to the lady in the back."

Me and the kids started cheering but the rest of the room was silent, and they all turned to look at us. So, we walked away embarrassed and I had to sign a bunch of paper work. I can't believe I bought my very own bakery. Things are moving along so fast. This must have been the right decision. It was a happy moment and I started to think that maybe things will be ok. The lady behind the desk gave me the keys so the kids and I went right over to check out the shop.

As we unlocked the door, everything was covered in white cloths. And upon removing them all, we saw that everything was in excellent condition. It had everything I could ever need down to the very last small fondant tool. I called momma right away to tell her the good news.

"I can't wait to see it." she said over the phone.

"Why don't you come up?" I suggested. "The grand opening is in a couple of weeks. I'd love for you to be here. "

"I have a better idea." momma stated. "Why don't I come ahead of time and help get things ready with you?"

"That would be great." I responded and the kids were thrilled as well.

A couple of days later, we picked up momma from the airport. Right away we went to the shop and she started telling us some of her ideas. She was proud of me and excited for this new chapter in our lives.

"Any word from...?" momma asked.

I knew she was talking about Jacob, so I answered, "He's texted and called a few times, but I never answer or respond."

She shook her head and continued to look around admiring everything that was left behind. We went back to our apartment and Bella gave her the grand tour. I decided to go get dinner ready since it was close to supper time. As we sat down to eat, momma was still trying to bring up Jacob.

"So," she began, "how are you?"

I thought for a minute than replied, "I'm good. Excited for the new bakery and this apartment is nice...." but then momma cut me off saying, "No Beth, how *are* you?"

I looked at her knowing she was wondering how I felt about what had happened before we moved here.

"She's miserable." Braydon said.

"I wouldn't say miserable." I responded surprised to hear him say that.

"Mom," he continued. "You cry in your sleep. I hear you. These walls are thin, you know."

I looked at Bella and she said, "It's true."

Then they all were just staring at me waiting for me to say something.

"I have a hard time sleeping." I said. "So sue me."

"Beth, it's ok to..." momma started but I immediately interrupted her loudly saying, "I know!"

Then there was silence. It was kind of awkward, so Braydon excused himself from the table and limped his way over to his room. He was finally off those crutches, but he still had a limp in his step. Bella said she was going to watch some tv and it was just me and momma left at the table. I sat there for a minute then I asked her.

"Has he been by?"

"Only about a million times." she responded.

I looked at her hoping she would say 'No he hasn't' because that would make this whole getting over him thing a lot easier. But secretly I wanted her to say that he was lost without me.

"He needs to get a life." I said angrily as I grabbed the dirty plates from the table to put them in the sink,

Momma got up and came over to me bringing the other dirty plates as well. She placed them in the sink and said to me, "He had one, it was you." Then she walked away.

I don't know what she expects of me. It's not like I can just pick up everything and go back. I just bought my very first bakery. The grand opening is next weekend. Braydon graduates high school next month. And my birthday is a couple months after that. I have too much going for me now to worry about Jacob. Although I must admit, I think about him every single day. Sometimes I think I see him walking down the street or driving in a car next to me. But it's always just my imagination. And then I remind myself that that's all he is, a fantasy, a fling from my past. I know that's not true but telling myself that makes me feel a little better. I have a feeling that once the shop is up and running, I won't have time to think about Jacob anymore. That's the plan anyway.

Chapter 14

It is grand opening day, and everything is chaos. I had hired a couple other people to work in the shop. And let me tell you what a task that's been. I thought it would be fun being my own boss and choosing people as my employees. But most people I interviewed seemed like they were either on drugs, completely irresponsible or just plain dumb. I'm not trying to be mean, but what happened to work ethic in America? I did manage to find a middle-aged woman named JoAnn Bliston and a young man named Mark Frederick who goes to school with Braydon. He's a very nice kid and seems to have a good head on his shoulders.

We all worked really hard making sure everything was just perfect. The crowd was beginning to line up outside and momma was putting the final finishing touches on some of the pastries. Even Bella helped by sweeping the floor. We were all there waiting for the clock to turn 10 a.m. The minutes ticked by and got louder and louder until finally, it was time.

"OK, let's open the doors." I said feeling anxious.

Braydon went and unlocked the doors and tons of people poured into the shop forming a line that went out the door and around the corner to the parking lot. I was amazed. There was even a local news station there to interview me. Apparently, the other bakeries in town only offer either cake or cupcakes or both. But we have pies and pastries and anything sweet you can think of. And it was a madhouse.

There were a couple times I swore I saw Jacob standing in line. But again, it was just my mind playing tricks on me. After the crowd died down, the bakery stayed busy all day with new customers consistently coming in and out. One time, I caught myself staring at what I thought was Jacob coming in the front entrance.

"What are you staring at?" Mark said to me.

I snapped out of my daydream and realized it was just Mark coming back in from taking out the trash.

"Sorry," I replied. "I thought I saw something."

I shook my head and went back to refilling the pastry tray. It was an astounding day. The bakery made more money in the first day then I could ever imagine. I only wish Jacob was here to experience this with me. But I know it's for the best. I am, what, 19 years older than him, about to be 20 years older? How would things be when I was old and grey at 70 years old and he's just turning 50? I have a feeling he'll be a devilishly handsome older man. I would probably look like a California raisin. I shuttered at the thought and closed up the register.

When Braydon went and locked the doors at the end of the day, I told everyone what I great job they did. We all clapped then I went around and high fived everyone.

"I wonder what tomorrow will be like?" Bella asked.

The 4 of us went back to the apartment to get cleaned up and relaxed the rest of the night. After the kids turned in and I helped momma make her bed on the couch, I thanked her for being here. She hugged me then I went and plopped on my bed. I kept thinking about Jacob and how I wished he would have been here today. I wondered what he was doing. I turned my head and noticed my phone was sitting on my nightstand. So I reached over and grabbed it. I may have deleted his name, but I still had all of our old messages. So, I scrolled through all my texts until I found a number with no name. I started to write a message telling him about the bakery and wishing he was here. But I slowly erased it one letter a time. Instead, I went and re-read all of the messages we ever sent each other. I smiled. I laughed. I started to cry. It was like reading a romantic comedy novel. I sighed and turned off my phone and decided to just change for bed. I had become aware that I cried myself to sleep in the past, so I made a strong, conscience effort not to cry that night.

The next 4 months went by really fast. Braydon has since graduated from high school and him and his friend Mark are working for me full time. On the morning of my birthday, I arrived at the shop a half hour before we were scheduled to open. Christine and I were the only ones there today. And after we opened the doors, it stayed pretty busy. When the day was coming to a close, Christine had clocked out and said her goodbyes. But then she stopped before she completely left the building.

"I almost forgot." she said. "I wanted to invite you to the Humble Pie tonight." That was a restaurant downtown.

"Um, yea. I might." I responded tired from the day.

"Come on. It'll be my treat?" Christine said trying to persuade me. "It's your birthday."

"Ok. You twisted my arm." I said to her agreeing to go.

We both smiled and said we'd see each other later. After I locked the doors, Bella and I headed back to the apartment to change and freshen up for the restaurant. Bella usually hangs out with me at the shop after school and sometimes helps with clean up. She says she wants to be a baker just like me when she grows up. On the way home, Braydon sent me a text and asked if it's ok if he hung out with Mark tonight. I agreed it was fine and told him to be careful.

"I'm glad to see Braydon made a new friend so quickly." I said to Bella.

"Yeah, me too." she replied.

Christine said the Humble Pie was kind of a chill place, so I put on a cute little white dress with sunflowers on it and white sandals. It was like any other birthday in my life, just going to dinner with people I care about. When we left the apartment though, I was feeling a little down. I still was thinking of Jacob and wondering what he was up to after all these months. I also wondered what he would have done for my birthday since he went all out for me on his birthday. Bella was talking to me the whole car ride there, but I didn't hear a word she said. I was completely zoned out in my own little world daydreaming about Jacob. I just couldn't believe that I still think about him every day. Moments later, we pulled up to the restaurant.

"Oh, it looks crowded." I said to myself.

We got out of the car and Bella grabbed my hand. But the second I walked through the doors that were surrounded by twinkle lights, I heard a large crowd of people yell "SURPRISE!" I was in total and complete shock. I began to get emotional as I saw many familiar faces smiling at me. There was Christine, that little sneak. There was Braydon and Mark and some other guys from his school. I saw momma, Peggy Sue and Billy Joe, Laura Lynn, Sue Ellen, Little Andy and his mom. So many people from Nashville Indiana came to celebrate my birthday. I couldn't believe my eyes. They also began to congratulate me on the bakery. I ran up to Peggy Sue and gave her the biggest hug.

"I can't believe you're here." I said feeling elated.

"I know right?" Peggy responded. "We all pitched in and got one of those Air B&B things."

"I'm so sorry I skipped town again." I told her getting choked up.

"Oh, fiddle sticks." she responded. "Things seem to be going well for you here."

We talked for a little bit about what's been going on the past few months back home. She mentioned she sees Jacob from time to time but always avoids him by going in the opposite direction. I made my rounds and said hello to everyone that had come and thanked them for making the trip. But there was one person I didn't see. Jacob. I was really wanting him to be there. But it's been months since I've seen him. He's probably moved on and is forgetting all about me.

Just then, Braydon and Mark were heading my way carrying a big cake with 40 candles. Everyone started singing which was something I wasn't accustomed too. When the guys placed the cake on the table in front of me, and after everyone was done singing, I made my wish and blew them all out. Everyone clapped and cheered.

"What did you wish for?" Bella asked.

I just smiled and answered, " I didn't wish for anything sweet pea. I have everything I need."

But that wasn't true. I actually wished for Jacob to be here with me right now.

"Mom?" Braydon began, "You promised you wouldn't lie anymore."

I looked at him confused knowing that I did lie about the wish but wondering how he would know that. I turned to Bella and with her sweet little voice said to me, "Maybe your wish will come true."

After she said that, she shifted her eyes to look behind me. I froze. I was wanting it to be Jacob but at the same time I didn't want to get my hopes up. My heart started beating faster and faster. Then I slowly turned around but kept looking at the floor the entire time. I saw a beat-up old pair of black doc martins so I slowly worked my way up the dark colored jeans to a teal colored button-down shirt. It was tucked in and the sleeves were rolled up. I saw flowers in someone's hand and right there behind them was that beautiful, gorgeous face of one Mr. Jacob Tyler Brooks. He also had on a white tie and the guitar pick tie clip I gave him in Washington. I gasped in shock and tears filled my eyes. He slowly walked up to me and handed me the large bouquet of sunflowers.

"Hello Elizabeth Harper." he said with his sexy voice.

"Jacob," I said softly then looked at Braydon. He smiled and I was so confused. I turned back to Jacob and asked, "How are you here?"

"I invited him." I heard Braydon say.

I turned around and just stared at my sweet boy. He smiled again and then winked at me.

"Beth?" Jacob said.

When I turned to look at Jacob, he was already down on one knee again. I covered my mouth with both hands completely stunned.

"I never got to finish asking you that question I wanted to ask." he said while looking up at me.

I started to cry but was so scared at the same time. I kept looking back at Braydon and he was actually smiling.

"Elizabeth Mary Harper." Jacob began, "I realized the moment I met you while you were holding my wallet at Hobnobs Corner, that you were going to be an important person in my life. But I had no idea that when I fell in love with you, I would also fall in love with your kids. Now, all of you are the most important people in my life."

He reached behind him and pulled out a small box from his back pocket then continued, "I have missed you terribly. And I don't want to spend another waking second without you. So.....will you do me the honor of saying yes to becoming my wife?"

Everyone in the room was watching this unfold.

"I don't understand." I said while crying and looking back to Bray. "How? When? How?"

I heard a few people in the crowd laugh at my expense. But then Braydon came up to me and said the sweetest thing, "I realized I was being selfish, mom. I didn't want to be the one to get in the way of your happiness while all you were doing was focusing on mine."

I smiled and tears were streaming down my face.

"I love you mom." Braydon continued. "Now will you answer the poor guy already?"

I laughed and turned my attention to Jacob. Then I looked at everyone in the room who were waiting for my answer to his question.

"Jacob?" I began. "I....." I paused for a moment and then I said something that shocked everyone, "I can't...."

Jacob looked devastated and held down his head. Everyone in the crowd let out a sad sigh. I just couldn't ruin his life like that. I already had my time. He needed to enjoy being young and not be tied down to someone with baggage like me.

"I'm sorry." I said as I started to cry harder.

I was so embarrassed. I had to get out of there as quick as I could. I humbly excused myself and made a run for the door.

"Mom?!" Braydon yelled as he began to follow me. But I didn't turn around.

"Mom! Wait!" Braydon said the moment I reached my car. "I thought this was what you wanted!"

I was really crying uncontrollably by that point, but I gained enough composure to turn around and say, "I can't do that to him Bray."

"Do what?" He asked.

"I can't have him waste his life on someone who's already lived theirs." I answered.

"Isn't that up to him to decide?" he maturely replied.

"He's right." I heard a voice from behind Braydon say. It was Jacob. As he came closer and closer to me, Braydon started to back away. "Being with you, being with your kids ... that's my choice."

"But...." I started to say but he wouldn't let me finish.

"But it's still my choice." He responded.

I just looked at him with tears in my eyes. Everyone was watching but I just couldn't say yes. So unfortunately, what came out of my mouth was, "I'm sorry. I just can't."

His eyes filled with tears this time and then I got in my car and drove off. As I was driving away, I heard Jacob, Braydon and my momma all taking turns calling my name to get me to stop. But I couldn't. I wasn't sure where I was going but I had to get out of there. I just kept driving until I came to a small bridge surrounded by trees over a small body of water. I pulled off to the side of the road and walked down to this lake. I sat on the ground at the edge of the lake and just cried. What is wrong with me? Braydon was right. Isn't this what I wanted? Isn't this what I wished for? Braydon invited him. So, he's definitely ok with this. All these thoughts bombarded my mind. I wasn't exactly sure why I said no. Is it really the age thing? Could this possibly work? I just feel unsure. The only thing I was sure of was how I felt about Jacob. But was love enough? I sat there for what felt like 30 minutes or so when my phone rang. It was Braydon. At first, I didn't want to pick up for fear it was Jacob calling me from Braydon's phone. But I answered and I heard Bray's voice on the other end.

"Are you ok?" He asked.

"No." I responded while crying.

"Where are you?"

"I found this spot. Just sitting here thinking."

"Can you please just come home and let's talk?" He asked so sincerely. "Please mom."

I thought for a second, that I asked him, "Did I just make a huge mistake?"

"Yes." He replied without hesitation. I was not expecting that. "But I'm sure it's not too late. Come home."

I quickly hung up the phone and ran to my car. Saying no was a mistake. I can feel it. I raced home as fast as I possibly could. Maybe Bray will take me to the airport, and we can catch up to Jacob so I can tell him how I really feel before it is too late. I arrived at my apartment and sprinted to the door. Once I opened it, I noticed not one single light was on but instead, the entire apartment was filled with lit candles everywhere I looked. There were rose pedals on the ground that went in one direction. And when I followed them to the end, there stood Jacob with his hands behind him looking scared and nervous.

"I thought I was too late." I said as I tried not to cry again.

He walked over to me and then so many people came from around the corner, from down the hall and from the kitchen. It was almost everyone from the restaurant. I couldn't believe my eyes. He stopped right in front of me and began to speak.

"So....we've been talking, " he began to say as he looked around the room at all the people there, "and we all came to the same conclusion. I'm not like most guys my age. Your friends, your family, they all think, and I agree with them, that you and I belong together." I smiled in laughter and tears started flowing. Then Jacob continued, "You are the one for me, Elizabeth. God made you for me. There is no doubt in my mind. I know exactly what I want, and it's something I've always wanted, a wife and family of my own."

"But I can't have any more children. I can't give you a family." I said to him softly while crying.

He then put his hands on my face and said to me while looking deep into my eyes, "You are my family."

That was the sweetest thing anyone has ever said to me. I couldn't help but get lost in his eyes and all I wanted to do was spend my life with this man. So, after taking a deep breath, I decided at that very moment, it was my time to be happy.

"Have you ever really looked at this?" I asked him still crying while touching his tie clip.

He looked down then back at me and quickly removed it. When he turned it over, he could see in very tiny print an engraving on the back that said, "I pick you."

He looked back up at me with a huge smile on his face then I said to him softly, "That's how I felt then and that's how I feel now."

His face lit up and he said, "So just so we're on the same page, does that mean you'll marry me?"

I nodded my head 'yes' vigorously and even said "Yes" out loud. He smiled that gorgeous, infectious smile of his and embraced me while the whole crowd went wild. Everyone started applauding and cheering for the both of us. He slipped a ring on my finger, looked me in the eyes and said, "I love you, Elizabeth Harper."

"I love you, Jacob Brooks." I replied. Then he put both his hands around my face and passionately kissed me for the longest time.

"I don't know if I'll ever get used to that." Braydon said in a joking way.

We all laughed then Braydon put his arms around me and Jacob. Bella then came and wrapped her arms around our waists. Then momma and everyone else came up to hug us and to congratulate us. It was a magical night. And I'm engaged to the man that I love. It all happened so quickly. I'm still in shock and speechless. But this man absolutely adores me. And I can't wait to see what the next chapter brings. So many thoughts ran through my head. Will we have a wedding? Will we have it here? Will I move back to Nashville? But then I realized that we have the rest of our lives to figure that out. One thing I do know is that for the first time in any of our lives, me and the kids are happy. We are all finally happy.

The

End

Made in the USA
Monee, IL
24 May 2025

cfaecf35-c41f-4add-a3eb-44208129893bR01